Oliver Thorne Miller

Upon the Tree-Tops

Oliver Thorne Miller

Upon the Tree-Tops

1st Edition | ISBN: 978-3-75243-791-1

Place of Publication: Frankfurt am Main, Germany

Year of Publication: 2020

Outlook Verlag GmbH, Germany.

Reproduction of the original.

UPON THE TREE-TOPS
BY
OLIVE THORNE MILLER

INTRODUCTORY.

In the beginning of my study of bird life, when I had a bird-room for close observation, I was interested to see that our little neighbors in feathers possess as much individuality of character as ourselves, and in Chapters XII. and XIII. of this volume I offer two studies of that period, illustrative of the point.

Thanks are due to Mr. Frederic A. Ober for the use of his notes on one of the solitaires, embodied in Chapter XII., and to the Godey Company for permission to reproduce two shrike pictures.

I wish also to give credit to my daughter, Mary Mann Miller, for the minute and conscientious collection of the facts recorded in Chapters V. and VI., which for convenience are related as if they were my own observations.

OLIVE THORNE MILLER.

I.

TRAMPS WITH AN ENTHUSIAST.

To a brain wearied by the din of the city, the clatter of wheels, the jingle of street cars, the discord of bells, the cries of venders, the ear-splitting whistles of factory and shop, how refreshing is the heavenly stillness of the country! To the soul tortured by the sight of ills it cannot cure, wrongs it cannot right, and sufferings it cannot relieve, how blessed to be alone with nature, with trees living free, unfettered lives, and flowers content each in its native spot, with brooks singing of joy and good cheer, with mountains preaching divine peace and rest!

Thus musing one evening, soon after my arrival at a lone farmhouse in the heart of the Green Mountains, I seated myself at the window to make acquaintance with my neighbors. Not the human; I wished for a time to turn away from the world of people, to find rest and recreation in the world outside the walls of houses.

My room was a wing lately added to the side of the cottage farthest from the life that went on in it, from the kitchen and dairy, from the sight of barns and henhouses. It was, consequently, as solitary as it could be, and yet retain a slight hold upon humanity. It was connected with the family and farm life by two doors, which I could shut at will, and be alone with nature, and especially with the beloved birds.

From my window I looked upon a wide view over the road and the green fields, and across the river to a lovely range of the Green Mountains, with one of the highest peaks in the State as a crown. Close at hand was a bank, the beginning of a mountain spur. It was covered from the road up with clumps of fresh green ferns and a few young trees,—a maple or two, half a dozen graceful young hemlocks, and others.

The top of the bank, about as high as my window, was thick with daisy buds, which I had caught that day beginning to open their eyes, sleepily, one lash at a time; and on looking closely I saw ranks of them still asleep, each yellow eye carefully covered with its snow-white fringes. When the blossoms were fully opened, a few days later, my point of view—on a level—made even

"The daisy's frill a wondrous newness wear;"

for I saw only the edges of the flower faces turned to the sky, while the stems

3

were visible down to the ground, and formed a Lilliputian forest in which it were easy to imagine tiny creatures spending days as secluded and as happy as I enjoyed in my forest of beech and birch and maple, which came down to the very back steps of the house.

FROM THE WINDOW.

On the evening when my story begins, early in June, I was sitting, as I said, at my window, listening to the good-night songs of the earlier birds, enjoying the view of woods and mountains, and waiting till tea should be over before taking my usual evening walk. I had fallen into a reverie, when I was aroused by the sound of wheels, and in a moment a horse appeared, trotting rapidly up the little hill. In his wake was a face. There was of course a body also, and some sort of a vehicle, but neither of them did I see; only a pair of eager, questioning eyes, and an intelligent countenance framed in snow-white curls which streamed back upon the wind,—a picture, a vision, I shall never forget.

I recognized at once my Enthusiast, a dear friend and fellow bird-lover, who I knew was coming to spend some weeks in the village. I rushed to the door to greet her.

"I'm delighted to see you!" she cried, as we clasped hands across the wheels. "I arrived an hour or two ago, and now I want to go where I can hear a hermit thrush. I've come all the way from Chicago to hear that bird."

She dismounted, declined the invitation to tea given by my hostess, who stood speechless with amazement at the erratic taste that would forego tea for the sake of a bird song, and we started at once up the road, where I had seen the bird perched in a partially dead hemlock-tree, and heard

> "his ravishing carol ring
> From the topmost twig he made his throne."

Everything was perfectly still. Not a bird peeped. Even the tireless vireo, who peopled the woods as the English sparrow the city streets, was hushed. I began to be anxious; could it be too cool for song? or too late? We walked steadily on, up the beautiful winding road: on one side dense forest, on the other lovely changing views of the hills across the intervale, blue now with approaching night. Crows called as they hurried over; the little sandpiper's "ah weet! weet! weet!" came up from the river bank, but in the woods all was silent.

Still we went on, climbing the steep hills, loitering through the valleys, till suddenly a bird note broke the stillness, quite near us, a low, yearning "wee-o!"

THE WONDERFUL SONG.

"The veery!" I whispered.

"Is that the veery?" she exclaimed. (She had come from the home of the wood thrush, where hermit and veery were unknown.)

"Yes," I said; "listen."

Again it came, more plaintive than before; once more, in an almost agonized tone; and so it continued, ever growing higher in pitch and more mournful, till we could hardly endure to listen to it. Then arose the matchless song, the very breath of the woods, the solemn, mysterious, wonderful song of the bird, and two listeners, at least, lingered in ecstasy to hear, till it dropped to silence again.

Then, slowly and leisurely, we went on. The dead hemlock, the throne of the hermit, was vacant. On a bank not far off we sat down to wait, talking in hushed tones of the veery, of the oven-bird whose rattling call was now just beginning, of the mysterious "see-here" bird whose plaintive call was sounding from the upper twig of another dead-topped tree, of the hermit himself, when, to our amazement, a small bird soared out of the woods, a few feet above our heads, flew around in a circle of perhaps fifteen feet in the air, and plunged again into the trees, singing all the time a rapturous, thrilling song, bewitching both in manner and in tone.

"The oven-bird!" we exclaimed in a breath. That made our walk noteworthy. We should not regret, even if the hermit refused to bless us.

Silently on up the road we passed, till the deepening shadows reminded us of the hour and the long drive before my friend, and we turned back. By this time the sun had set, and the sky was filled with gorgeous rosy clouds floating above the richest red-purple of the mountains. This surely crowned our walk.

We were sauntering homeward, lingering, waiting, we hardly knew for what, since we had given up the hermit, when a single bird note arrested me. Then, as his first rich clause fell upon the air, I turned to my companion, who was a few steps behind me. She stood motionless, both hands raised, but dumb.

"Glorious!" she whispered when she recovered her voice. "Wonderful!" she added, as he warmed into fuller song.

Quietly drawing as near as we dared, we dropped upon the bank and listened in spellbound silence to our unseen melodist. Slow, rapturous, entrancing was his song; and when it ended we came reluctantly back to earth, stole in the growing darkness down to the farm, and my friend resumed her place in the carriage and drove away, saying with her good-by, "I am already paid for my long journey."

Yet after the first surprise and wonder were over, she swung loyally back to her first love, the wood thrush, of whose sublime voice she says, "The first solemn opening note transports you instantly into a holy cathedral."

For myself, I have never been able to choose permanently between these two glorious singers, and at that time I had been under the spell of the hermit song for days. Morning after morning I had spent in the woods, listening to the marvelous voice, and trying to discover its charm.

The bird began to sing his way down to us about ten o'clock in the morning. I heard him first afar off, then coming nearer and nearer, till he reached some favorite perch in the woods behind, and very near the farmhouse, before noon, where he usually sang at intervals till eight o'clock in the evening. I studied his song carefully. It consisted of but one clause, composed of a single emphasized note followed by two triplets on a descending scale. But while retaining the relative position of these few notes he varied the effect almost infinitely, by changing both the key and the pitch constantly, with such skill

that I was astonished to discover the remarkable simplicity of the song. A striking quality of it was an attempt which he frequently made to utter his clause higher on the scale than he could reach, so that the triplets became a sort of trill or tremolo, at the very extreme of his register. Sometimes he gave the triplets alone, without the introductory note; but never, in the weeks that I studied his song, did he sing other than this one clause.

It was only with an effort that I could force myself to analyze the performance. Far easier were it, and far more delightful, to sit enchanted, to be overwhelmed and intoxicated by his thrilling music. For me, the hermit voices the sublimity of the deep woods, while the veery expresses its mystery, its unfathomable remoteness. A wood warbler, on the contrary, always brings before me the rush and hurry of the world of people, and the wood pewee its under-current of eternal sadness. Into the mood induced by the melancholy pewee song breaks how completely and how happily the cheery optimism of the chickadee! Brooding thoughts are dissipated, all is not a hollow mockery, and life is still worth living.

A PERFECT NOOK.

Often, when listening to the hermit song, I wondered that at the first note of the king of singers all other birds were not mute. But evidently the birds have not enthroned this thrush. Possibly, even, they do not share human admiration for his song. The redstart goes on jerking out his monotonous ditty; chippy irreverently mounts a perch and trills out his inane apology for a song; the vireo in yonder tree spares us not one of his never-ending platitudes. But the hermit thrush goes on with sublime indifference to the voices of common folk down below. Sometimes he is answered from afar by another of his kind, who arranges his notes a little differently. The two seem to wait for each other, as if not to mar their divine harmony by vulgar haste or confusion.

"We must find the 'see-here' bird," said my friend the next morning, when she appeared at the door of the farmhouse, and I joined her for our second tramp. This was a bird whose long, deliberate notes, sounding like the above words, had tantalized me from the day of my arrival.

We resolved this time to go into the woods we had skirted the night before. A set of bars admitted us to a most enticing bit of forest, a paradise to city-weary eyes and nature-loving hearts. From the bars rose sharply a rough wood road, while a few steps to the right and a scramble up a rocky path changed the whole world in a moment. We were in a perfect nook, which I had discovered a few days before, with a carpet of dead leaves, a sky of waving branches, the fierce sun shut out by curtains of living green, the air cooled by a clear mountain stream, and the "priceless gift of delicious silence"—silence that had haunted my dreams for months—broken only by the voices of birds, whispers of leaves, and ripple of brook. In this spot,

> "where Nature dwells alone,
> Of man unknowing, and to man unknown,"

(as I tried to persuade myself) I had established my out-of-door study, and here I had spent perfect days, watching the residents of the vicinity, and saturating my whole being with the delights of sight and sound and scent till it was thrilling happiness just to be alive. Would that I could impart the freshness, the fragrance, the heavenly peace of those days to this chronicle, to comfort and strengthen my readers not so blessed as to share them!

The dwellers in this delectable spot, where I persuaded my friend to rest a moment, I had not found altogether what I should have chosen; for, unfortunately, the place most desirable for the student is not always the best for birds. They are quite apt to desert the cool, breezy heights charming to wood-lovers, to build in some impenetrable tangle, where the ground is wet and full of treacherous quagmires, where mosquitoes abound, and flies do greatly flourish, where close-growing branches and leaves keep out every breath of air, and there is no solid rest for the legs of a camp-stool. Such a difference does it make, as to a desirable situation, from which side you look at it.

A SPORTSMAN IN FUR.

The principal inhabitant presented himself before we were fairly seated, a

7

chipmunk, who came out of his snug door under the roots of a maple-tree and sat up on his doorstep—one of the roots—to make his morning toilet, dress his sleek fur, scent the sweet fresh air, and enjoy himself generally. In due time he ran down to the little brook before the door, and then started out, evidently after something to eat; and he went nosing about on the ground with a thoroughness to make a bird-lover shudder, for what ground bird's nest could escape him!

I recognize the fact that, from his point of view, chipmunks must live, and why should they not have eggs for breakfast? Doubtless, in squirrel philosophy, it is a self-evident truth that birds were created to supply the tables of their betters in fur, and the pursuit of eggs and nestlings adds the true sportsman's zest to the enjoyment of them. So long, therefore, as the law that "might makes right" prevails in higher quarters, we are forced to acknowledge, however grudgingly, his "right" to his game; but for all that I should like exceedingly to protect it from him.

I could not long keep a bird-lover studying a chipmunk. In a few minutes we started again on our way up the mountain. Each side of our primitive wood road was bordered with ferns in their first tender green, many of them still wearing their droll little hoods. Forward marched the Enthusiast; breathlessly I followed. Up one little hill, down another, over a third we hastened.

"See!" I said, hoping to arrest the tireless steps; "on that tree I saw yesterday a scarlet tanager."

"Oh, did you?" she said carelessly, pausing not an instant in her steady tramp.

Then rose the note we were listening for, far to the left of the road.

"He's over there!" she cried eagerly, leaving the path, and pushing in the direction of the sound. "But I'm afraid I shall tire you," she added. "You sit down here, and I'll just go on a little."

"No, indeed!" I answered hastily, for I knew well what "just go on a little" meant,—I had tried it before: it meant pass out of sight in two minutes, and out of hearing in one more, so absorbed in following an elusive bird note that everything else would be forgotten. "No, indeed!" I repeated. "I shall not be left in these woods; where you go I follow."

"But I won't go out of sight," she urged, her conscience contending with her eager desire to proceed, for well she knew that I did not take my woods by storm in this way.

AN ECCENTRIC FOX.

I said nothing in reply, but I had no intention of being left, for I did not know what dwellers the forest might contain, and I had a vivid remembrance of being greatly startled, only a day or two before, by unearthly cries in these

8

very woods; of seeing a herd of young cattle rushing frantically away, turning apprehensive glances toward the sounds, and huddling in a frightened heap down by the bars, while the strange cries came nearer and nearer, till I should not have been surprised to see any sort of a horror emerge; of calling out to the farmer whom I met at the door, "Oh, there's something dreadful up in the woods!" and his crushing reply, "Yes, I heard it. It's a fox barking; we hear one now and then."

I cast no doubts on the veracity of that farmer, though I could not but remember the license men sometimes allow themselves when trying to quiet fears they consider foolish; nor did his solution seem to account satisfactorily for the evident terror of the cattle, which had lived in those woods all their lives, and had no reason to fear the "bark" of a fox. I preferred, therefore, not to encounter any such eccentric "fox" alone; hence I refused to listen to my friend's entreaties, but simply followed on, over fallen tree-trunks, under drooping branches, and through unyielding brush; now sinking ankle-deep in a pile of dead leaves, now catching my hair in a broken branch, and now nearly falling over a concealed root; wading through swamps, sliding down banks, cutting and tearing our shoes, and leaving bits of our garments everywhere. On we went recklessly, intent upon one thing only,—seeing the bird who, enthroned on his tree-top, calmly and serenely uttered his musical "see-e he-e-re!" while we struggled and scrambled and fought our way down below.

We reached a steep bank, and paused a moment, breathless, disheveled, *my* interest in the beguiler long ago cooled.

"There's a brook down there," I said hastily; "we can't cross it."

Could we not? But we did, at the expense of a little further rending, and the addition of wet feet to our other discomforts. But at last! at last! we came in sight of our bird, a mere black speck against the sky.

"It's a flycatcher!" exclaimed my companion eagerly. "See his attitude! I must get around the other side!" and on we went again. A fence loomed before us, a fence of brush, impossible to get through, and almost as impossible to get over. But what were any of man's devices to an eager bird-hunter! Over that fence she went—like a bird, I was going to say, but like a boy would perhaps be better. More leisurely and with difficulty I followed, for once on the other side I should be content. I knew the road could not be far off, and through the tangled way we had come I was resolved I would not pass again.

UPON THE TREE-TOP.

Well, we ran him down. He was obliging enough to stay in one spot, indifferent to our noisy presence on the earth below, while we studied him on all sides, and decided him to be the olive-sided flycatcher (*Contopus*

9

borealis). We entered his name and his manners in our notebooks, and we were happy, or at least relieved.

The habit of this bird, as I learned by observation of him afterward, was to sit on the highest twig of a tree dead at the top, where he could command a view of the whole neighborhood, and sing or call by the hour, in a loud, drawling, and rather plaintive tone, somewhat resembling the wood pewee's, though more animated in delivery. I found that the two notes which syllabled themselves to my ear as "see-e he-e-re!" were prefaced by a low, staccato utterance like "quick!" and all were on the same note of the musical scale. Occasionally, but not often, he made a dash into the air, flycatcher fashion, and once I saw him attempt to drive away a golden-winged woodpecker who took the liberty of alighting on a neighboring dead tree-trunk. Down upon him like a small tornado came the flycatcher instantly, expecting, apparently, to annihilate him. But the big, clumsy woodpecker merely slid one side a little, to avoid the onslaught, and calmly went on dressing his feathers as if no small flycatcher existed. This indifference did not please the olive-sided, but he alighted on a branch below and bided his time; it came soon, when the goldenwing took flight, and he came down upon him like a kingbird on a crow. I heard the snap of the woodpecker's beak as he passed into the thick woods, but nobody was hurt, and the flycatcher returned to his perch.

When we had rested a little after our mad rush through the woods, we found that the hours were slipping away, and we must go. Passing down the road at the edge of the woods, we were about to cross a tiny brook, when our eyes fell upon a distinguished personage at his bath. He was a rose-breasted grosbeak, and we instantly stopped to see him. He did not linger, but gave himself a thorough splashing, and flew at once to a tree, where he began dressing his plumage in frantic haste, as if he knew he was a "shining mark" for man and beast. He stayed half a minute on one branch, jerked a few feathers through his beak, then flew to another place and hurriedly dressed a few more; and so he kept on, evidently excited and nervous at being temporarily disabled by wet feathers, though I do not think he knew he had human observers, for we were at some distance and perfectly motionless. He was a beauty, even for his lovely family, and the rose color of his wing-linings was the most gorgeous I ever saw.

DRESSING IN A HURRY.

Moreover, I knew this bird, later, to be as useful as he was beautiful. He it was who took upon himself the care of the potato-patch in the garden below, spending hours every day in clearing off the destructive potato-beetle, singing as he went to and from his labors, and, when the toils of the day were over, treating us to a delicious evening song from the top of a tree close by.

In that way the grosbeak's time was spent till babies appeared in the hidden

10

nest, when everything was changed, and he set to work like any hod-carrier; appearing silently, near the house, on the lowest board of the fence, looking earnestly for some special luxury for baby beaks. No more singing on the tree-tops, no more hunting of the beetle in stripes; food more delicate was needed now, and he found it among the brakes that grew in clumps all about under my window. It was curious to see him searching, hopping upon a stalk which bent very much with his weight, peering eagerly inside; then on another, picking off something; then creeping between the stems, going into the bunch out of sight, and reappearing with his mouth full; then flying off to his home. This bird was peculiarly marked, so that I knew him. The red of his breast was continued in a narrow streak down through the white, as if the color had been put on wet, and had dripped at the point.

The third tramp with my Enthusiast was after a warbler. To my fellow bird-students that tells a story. Who among them has not been bewitched by one of those woodland sprites, led a wild dance through bush and brier, satisfied and happy if he could catch an occasional glimpse of the flitting enchanter!

This morning we drove a mile or two out of the village, hitched our horse,—a piece of perfection, who feared nothing, never saw anything on the road, and would stand forever if desired,—and started into the pasture. The gate passed, we had first to pick our way through a bog which had been cut by cows' hoofs into innumerable holes and pitfalls, and then so overgrown by weeds and moss that we could not always tell where it was safe to put a foot. We consoled ourselves for the inconvenience by reflecting that a bog on the side of a mountain must probably be a provision of Mother Nature's, an irrigating scheme for the benefit of the hillside vegetation. If all the water ran off at once, we argued, very little could grow there. So we who love to see our hills covered with trees should not complain, but patiently seek the stepping-stones sometimes to be found, or meekly resign ourselves to going in over boot-tops without a word.

THE HERMIT'S NEST.

Our first destination was the nest of a hermit thrush, discovered by my friend the day before; and we stumbled and slipped and picked our way a long distance over the dismal swamp, floundering on till we reached a clump of young hemlocks, on ground somewhat more solid, where we could sit down to rest. There was the nest right before us, a nicely made, compact bird home, exquisitely placed in one of the little trees, a foot from the ground.

While waiting for the owners to appear, I was struck with the beauty of the young hemlocks, so different from most evergreen trees. From the time a hemlock has two twigs above ground it is always picturesque in its method of growth. Its twigs, especially the topmost one, bend over gracefully like a plume. There is no rigid uniformity among the smaller branches, no two appear to be of the same length, but there is an artistic variety that makes of the little tree a thing of beauty. When it puts out new leaves in the early summer, and every twig is tipped with light green, it is particularly lovely, as if in bloom.

How different the mathematical precision of the spruce, which might indeed have been laid out upon geometrical lines! When a baby spruce has but three twigs, one will stand stiffly upright, as if it bore the responsibility of upholding the spruce traditions of the ages, while the other twigs will duly spread themselves at nearly right angles, leaving their brother to represent the aspirations of the family, and thus even in infancy reproduce in miniature the full-grown, formal tree.

When, after waiting some time in vain for the birds to appear, we examined the nest before us, we found that it held two thrush eggs and one of the cowbird. The impertinence of this disreputable bird in thrusting her plebeian offspring upon the divine songster, to rear at the expense of her own lovely brood, was not to be tolerated. The dirty speckled egg looked strangely out of place among the gems that belonged to the nest, and I removed it, careful not to touch nest or eggs. So pertinacious is this parasite upon bird society that my friend says that in Illinois, where the wood thrush represents the charming family, almost every wood thrush nest, in the early summer, contains a cowbird's egg; and not until they have reared one of the intruders can the birds hope to have a brood of their own. Fortunately they nest twice in the season, and the cowbird does not disturb the second family.

While we sat watching the hermit's nest, we were attracted by another resident of that cozy group of hemlocks and maples. He appeared upon a low shrub within twenty feet of us, and began to sing. First came a long, deliberate note of the clearest and sweetest tone, then two similar notes, a third higher, followed by three triplets on the same note. Though dressed in sparrow garb, his colors were bright, and he was distinguished and made really beautiful by two broad lines of buff-tinted white over his crown, and a snowy white throat. He was the white-throated sparrow, one of the largest and most interesting of his family. The charm of his song is its clearness of tone and deliberateness of utterance. It is calm as the morning, finished, complete, and almost the only bird song that can be perfectly imitated by a human whistle. I never shared the enthusiasm of some of my fellow bird-lovers for the sparrows till I knew the white-throat and learned to love the dear little song sparrow. It is unfortunate that the song of the former has been translated into a word so unworthy as "peabody," and that the name "peabody bird" has become fastened on him in New England. Far more appropriate the words applied by Elizabeth Akers Allen to an unknown singer,—possibly this very bird,—embodied in her beautiful poem "The Sunset Thrush." For whatever bird it was intended, the syllables and arrangement correspond to the white-throat's utterance, and the words are, "Sweet! sweet! sweet! Sorrowful! sorrowful! sorrowful!"

A white-throat who haunted the neighborhood of my farmhouse did not confine himself to the family song; which, by the way, varies less with this species than with any other I know. At first, for some time, he entirely omitted the triplets, making his song consist of four long notes, the fourth being in place of the triplets. Then, later, he dropped the last note a half tone below the others, still omitting the triplets, which, in fact, in three or four weeks of listening and watching, I never once heard him utter. In July of that year, in passing over the Canadian Pacific Railway on my way West, I heard innumerable songs by this bird. Every time the train stopped, white-throat voices rang out on all sides, and with considerable variety. Many dropped half a tone at the end, and some uttered the triplets on that note, while others began the song on a higher note, and gave the rest a third below, instead of above, as usual.

FINDING BIRDS'-NESTS.

But to return to the singer before us on that memorable day. After singing a long time, he suddenly began to utter the first two notes alone, and then apparently to listen. We also listened, and soon heard a reply of the same two notes on a different pitch. These responsive calls were kept up for some time, and seemed to be signals between the bird and his mate; for neither she nor her nest could be found, though the pair had been startled out of that very bush on the preceding day. We searched the clumps of shrubs carefully, but without success.

I long ago came to the conclusion that the ability to find nests easily is as truly a natural gift as the ability to become a musician, or the power to see a statue in a block of marble. That gift is not mine. I have an almost invincible repugnance to poking into bushes and thrusting aside branches to discover who has hidden there. Moreover, if a bird seems anxious or alarmed, I never can bear to disturb her. Nor indeed do I care to find many nests. A long list of nests found in a season gives me no pleasure; how many birds belong to a certain district does not concern me in the least. But if I have really studied one or two nests, and made acquaintance with the tricks and manners of the small dwellers therein, I am satisfied and happy.

While we lingered in the little hemlock grove, enraptured with the white-throat, and feeling that

"Here were the place to lie alone all day
On shadowed grass, beneath the blessed trees,"

a distant note reached our ever-listening ears. It was the voice of a warbler, and a most alluring song. Such indeed we found it, for on the instant the Enthusiast sprang to her feet, alert to her finger-tips, crying, "That's the bird we're after!" adding as usual, as she started across the field, "You sit still! I won't go far," while as usual, also, I snatched my things and followed.

The song was in the tone of one of the most bewitching as well as the most elusive of warblers, the black-throated green; a bird not so big as one's thumb, with a provoking fondness for the tops of the tallest trees, where foliage is thickest, and for keeping in constant motion, flitting from twig to twig, and from tree to tree, throwing out as he goes

"The sweetest sound that ever stirred
A warbler's throat."

This one was tireless, as are all of his tribe, and led us a weary dance over big, steep-sided rocks, through more and more bogs, over a fence, and out of our open fields into deep woods.

"YOU SIT STILL."

Now, my companion in these tramps has a rooted opinion that she is easily fatigued, and must rest frequently; and I have no doubt it is true, when she has no strong interest to urge her on. So she used to burden herself with a clumsy waterproof, to throw on the ground to sit upon; and in compliance with this notion (which was most amusing to those whom she tired out in her tramps), whenever she thought of it—that is, when the bird voice was still for a

14

moment—she would seek a sloping bank, or a place beside a tree where she could lean, and then throw herself down, determined to rest. But always in one minute or less, the warbler would be sure to begin again, when away went good resolutions and fatigue, and she sprang up like a Jack-in-the-box, saying, of course, "You sit still; I'll just go on a little," and off we went over brake and brier.

While pursuing this vocal *ignis fatuus* I made a charming discovery. In one of the temporary pauses in our wild career, I was startled by the flight of a bird from the ground very near us, and, searching about, I soon found a veery's nest with one egg. It was daintily placed in a clump of brakes or big ferns, resting on a fallen stick, over and around which the brakes had grown.

The bird was not so pleased with my discovery as I was. She perched on a tree over our heads, and uttered the mournful veery cry; and though I did not so much as lay a finger on that nest, I believe she deserted it at that moment, for several days afterward it was found exactly as on that day, with its one egg cold and abandoned.

If I had not, through two summers' close study, made myself very familiar with the various calls and cries of the veery, I think I should be driven wild by them; for no bird that I know can impart such distance to his notes, and few can get around so silently and unobserved as he. A great charm in his song is that it rarely bursts upon your notice; it appears to steal into your consciousness, and in a moment the air seems full of his breezy, woodsy music, his "quivering, silvery song," as Cheney calls it.

Not long were we allowed to meditate upon the charms of the veery, for again the luring song began, the other side of the belt of woods, and off we started anew. This time we secured the bird, or his name, which was all we desired. The sweet beguiler turned out to be the warbler mentioned above, the black-throated green, but with a more than usually exquisite arrangement of his notes. Indeed, my friend, who was what I call warbler-mad,—a state of infatuation I have with care and difficulty guarded myself against,—heard in the woods of the neighborhood, during that summer's visit, no less than four different songs from the same species of warbler.

THE LAST TRAMP.

While slowly and weariedly dragging myself back to where our patient horse stood waiting, I fell into meditation on this way of making the study of nature hard work instead of rest and refreshment, and the comparative merits of chasing up one's birds and waiting for them to come about one. Without doubt the choice of method is due largely to temperament, but I think it will be found that most of our nature-seers have followed the latter course.

June was now drawing to an end, and the day of my friend's departure had nearly arrived. One more tramp remained to us. It was a walk up a long, lonely road to a solitary thorn-tree, where I was studying a shrike's nest.

Just as we left the village a robin burst into song, and this bird, because of certain associations, was the Enthusiast's favorite singer. We paused to listen. When bird music begins to wane, when thrushes have taken their broods afar, and orioles and catbirds are heard no more, one appreciates the hearty philosophy, the cheerful and pleasing song, of the robin. It is truly delightful then to hear his noisy challenge, his gleeful "laugh," his jolly song. We may indeed rhapsodize over our rare, fine singers, but after all we could better spare one and all of them than our two most common songsters, our faithful stand-bys, upon whom we can always count to preach to us the gospel of contentment, cheerfulness, and patience,—the dear common robin and the blessed little song sparrow. No weather is so hot that they will not pour out their evangel to us; no rain so wet, no wind so strong, that these two will not let their sweet voices be heard. Blessed, I say, be the common birds, living beside our dwellings, bringing up their young under our very eyes, accepting our advances in a spirit of friendliness, coming earliest, staying latest, and keeping up their song even through the season of feeding, when many become silent. These two are indispensable to us; these two should be dearest to us; these, above all others, should our children be taught to respect and love.

The robin ceased, and we passed on. One more voice saluted us from the last house of the village: a wren, whose nest was placed in a bracket under the roof, sang his gushing little ditty, and then in a moment we were in a different bird world. From one side came the bobolink's voice,

"Preaching boldly to the sad the folly of despair,
And telling whom it may concern that all the world is fair;"

from the other, the plaintive notes of the meadow lark.

THE LARK'S "SPUTTER."

Lovely indeed the lark looked among the buttercups in the pasture, stretching himself up from the ground, tall and slim, and almost as yellow as they; and very droll his sputtering cry, as he flew over the road to the deep grass of the meadow, to attend to the wants of his family, for the meadow was full of mysterious sounds under the grass, and seemed to give both bobolink and lark much concern.

The call I name the "sputter," because it sounds like nothing else on earth, is a sort of "retching" note followed by several sputtering utterances, hard to describe, but not unpleasant to hear, perhaps because it suggests the meadow under the warm sun of June, with bobolinks soaring and singing, and a populous colony beneath the long grass. Now night was coming on, and the larks were passing from the pasture, where they seemed to spend most of the day, some with song and some with sputter, over the road, to drop into the grass and be seen no more;

"While through the blue of the sky the swallows, flitting and flinging,
Sent their slender twitterings down from a thousand throats."

Sometimes, on that lonely road, which I passed over several times a day, I was treated to a fairy-like sight. It was when a recent shower had left little puddles in the clay road, and the eave swallows from a house across the meadow came down to procure material for their adobe structures. Most daintily they alighted on their tiny feet around the edge, holding up their tails like wrens, lest they should soil a feather of their plumage, and raising both wings over their backs like butterflies, fluttering them all the time, as if to keep their balance and partly hold them up from the ground,—a lovely sight which I enjoyed several times.

Under the eaves of the distant house, where the nests of these birds were placed, and which I visited later, were evidences of tragedies. The whole length of the cornice on the back side of the house showed marks of many nests, and there were left at that time but four, two close together at each end of the line. I cannot say positively that the nests had fallen while in use, but in another place, a mile away, I know of a long row having fallen, with young in, every one of whom was killed. Where was the "instinct" of the birds whose hopes thus perished? And was the trouble with their material or with their situation? I noticed this: that the nests had absolutely nothing to rest on, not even a projecting board. They were plastered against a perfectly plain painted board.

THE PHŒBE'S TALK.

Another bird whom I caught in a new rôle, apparently giving a lesson in food-hunting to a youngster, was a phœbe. Hearing a new and strange cry, mingled with tones of a voice familiar to me, I looked up, and discovered a young and an old phœbe. The elder kept up a running series of remarks in the tone peculiar to the species, while the infant answered, at every pause, by a querulous single note in a higher key. Every moment or two the instructor would fly out and capture something, talking all the while, as if to say, "See how easy it is!" but careful not to give the food to the begging and complaining pupil. No sooner did the parent alight than the youngster was after him, following him everywhere he went. After a while the old bird flew away, when that deceiving little rogue took upon himself the business of fly-catching. He flew out, snapped his beak, and, returning to his perch, wiped it carefully. Yet when the elder returned he at once resumed his begging and crying, as if starved and unable to help himself.

A friend and bird-student, whose home is in these mountains, assures me that the phœbes in this vicinity do not confine themselves to the traditional family cry, but have a really pleasing song, which she has heard several times. That, then, is another of the supposed songless birds added to the list of singers. I know both the kingbird and the wood pewee sing, not, to be sure, in a way to be compared to the thrushes, though far excelling the utterances of the warblers. But why are they so shy of exhibiting their talent? Why do they make such a secret of it? Can it be that they are just developing their musical abilities?

When we reached the thorn-tree, on that last evening, we seated ourselves on the bank beside the road, to enjoy the music of the meadow, and to see the shrike family. At the nest all was still, probably settled for the night, but the "lord and master" of that snug homestead stood on a tall maple-tree close by, in dignified silence, watching our movements, no doubt. We waited some time, but he refused either to go or to relax his vigilance in the least, till the hour grew late, and we were obliged to turn back.

The sun had set, and the sky was filled, as on that first evening, with soft, rosy sunset clouds, and the distant mountains, with Jay Peak for a crown, were clothed in gorgeous purple again. With all this beauty before us, we slowly walked back to the village, and I felt it a fitting close to my delightful if exhausting tramps with an Enthusiast.

II.

A MYSTERIOUS STRANGER.

My first sight of the little stranger was one morning when returning from a long stroll in search of a nest of the red-headed woodpecker. It was not through the woods I had been, as might be expected. I did not search the dead limbs or lifeless trees; on the contrary, I followed the dusty road and examined the telegraph poles, for the woodpecker of these latter days has departed from the ways of his fathers, deserted the cool and fragrant woods, and taken up his abode in degenerate places, a fitting change of residence to follow his change of habit from digging his prey out of the tree-trunks to catching it on the wing.

On this special morning I found holes enough, and birds enough, but no hole that seemed to belong to any particular bird; and as I walked along home by the railroad, I came upon my little stranger. He was seated comfortably, as it appeared, on a telegraph wire, so comfortably, indeed, that he did not care to disturb himself for any stray mortal who might chance to pass.

I stopped to look, and hurriedly note his points, fearing every moment that he would take wing; but not a feather stirred. A king on his throne could not be more absolutely indifferent to a passer-by than this little beauty. He was self-possessed as a thrush, and serene as a dove, but he was not conveniently placed for study, being above my head in strong sunlight, against a glaring sky. I could see only that his under parts were beautiful fluffy white dusted with blue-gray, and that he had black on the wings. He was somewhat smaller than a robin, and held his tail with the grace of a catbird.

On several subsequent days I passed that way frequently, sometimes seeing the bird alone, again with a comrade, but always noting the same reserved and composed manners, and always so placed that I could not see his markings. It was not until a week or ten days later that I had a more satisfactory view.

I was taking my usual afternoon walk, about five o'clock, when, as I approached a little pond beside the road, up started the unknown from a brush heap on the edge. He flew across the road to a tree near the track, and I was about to follow him when my eye fell upon another on the fence beyond, and on walking slowly toward him I discovered a second, and then a third. Three of the beauties on a fence a little way apart—there was then a family! I stood and gazed.

The backs and heads of the birds, as I could then plainly see, were a little darker shade of the delicate blue-gray, with the same soft, fluffy look I had noticed on the breast. The wings were black and somewhat elaborately marked with white. The beak, that tell-tale feature which reveals the secret of a bird's life, was not long, but thick, and black as jet, and the dark eye was set in a heavy, black band across the side of the head. The combination of black and gray was very effective, and closer acquaintance did not modify my first opinion of the little stranger; he was a bonny bird with clear, open gaze, graceful in every movement, and innocent and sweet in life I was sure, and am still, in spite of—

But let me tell my story: While I was noting these things I heard the cries of a bird-baby behind me. The voice was strange to me, and of a curiously human quality. I turned hastily, and there on the telegraph pole was the baby in gray, receiving his supper from one of his parents, and crying over it, as do many feathered little folk—one more of the mysterious family.

There were thus five in sight at once, and at least three of them were infants lately out of the nest, hardly taught to feed themselves; yet the most sedate head of the household was no more dignified and grown-up in manner than was the youngest of them, for when he had cried over his repast and descended to the fence I could not tell him from Mamma herself.

I soon discovered that this was no junketing party; all were on business bent. They might look at me and they did, although I was not near enough to disturb them; but each and every one kept at least one eye on the ground, where were growing beans or some plant about three inches high, and I'm sure no small creature could stir in that part of the world that one of those sharp eyes did not light upon it. They were ten or fifteen feet apart, so that each had his own share of territory to overlook, and every few moments one flew to the ground, seized something, and returned at once to his place, ready for another. It was a wire fence, and they always selected the wires instead of the posts to perch upon. Sitting and never standing, their attitude expressed the most charming serenity.

While I stood watching, two of the youngsters happened to pounce upon the same object,—a worm it looked like,—and there was for a moment a spirited tug of war. Each held on to his end, and resisted with cries the attempts of his brother to deprive him of it. Doubtless the prey, whatever it was, suffered in this affair, for in a moment they separated amicably, and each returned to his station on the fence. These three were babies; their actions betrayed them; for a little later, when one of the elders flew from the field to a low peach-tree, instantly there arose the baby-cry "ya-a-a-a!" and those three sedate looking personages on the wire arose as one bird, and flew to the tree, alighting almost on the mother, so eager were they to be fed. In a moment she flew to the fence, where all three followed her. When she escaped from their importunities she came much nearer to me, doubtless to see if I needed watching, and I had a closer look than I had succeeded in getting before, and satisfied myself on a point or two of marking.

Up to this time my searching into the name and identity of my little strangers in gray had been in vain. But a direful suspicion was growing within me. That heavy black line from the eye! The strongly marked wings! I turned with dread to a family I had not thought of trying—the shrikes. There were the markings, too true! But that delicate blue-gray was not "slate color." Still, people see colors differently, and in every other way the description was perfect. They must be—my beautiful, graceful, attractive strangers must be— butcher-birds!

Dreadful discovery! I must at once know all about them; whether they deserve the name and the reputation. I flew to my books.

"The character of the butcher-bird," says Wilson, "is entitled to no common degree of respect. His courage and intrepidity are beyond every other bird of his size, and in affection for his young he is surpassed by no other. He attacks the largest hawk or eagle in their defense with a resolution truly astonishing, so that all of them respect him;" and, further, "He is valued in Carolina and Georgia for the destruction of mice. He sits on the fence and watches the stacks of rice, and darts upon them, also destroying grasshoppers and crickets."

So said Wilson, but subsequent writers have said terrible things about him: that he catches small birds and impales them on thorns; that he delights in killing more than he can eat. Could these things be true? Where, then, was the larder of this family? Such a curious and wonderful place I must see. I resolved to devote myself to discovering the secrets of this innocent looking family in gray.

A THORNY MONSTER.

The nest where they had first seen the light was in a low spruce-tree beside a constantly used gate, not more than eight feet from the ground, and across the road was a tree they much frequented. Next to that, and overshadowed by it, was, as I now discovered, a thorny tree, "honey locust" it is called. Ominous proximity! I resolved to investigate. Perhaps I should find the birds' place of storage. I crossed the track and went to the tree. What a structure it was! A mere framework for thorns, and a finer array of them it would be hard to find, from the tiny affair an inch in length, suitable to hold a small grasshopper, to foot-long spikes, big enough to impale a crow. Not only was every branch and every twig bristling with them, but so charged was the whole tree with the "feeling" of thorns, that it actually sent out great clumps of them from the bare trunk, where there was not a shadow of excuse for being. They grew in a confused mass, so that at first I thought there had been a hole which some person had stopped by crowding it full of those vegetable needles, at all angles, and of all sizes up to the largest. On one side alone of the trunk, not more than five feet high, were eight of these eruptions of thorns. Could the most bloodthirsty shrike desire a more commodious larder?

22

I looked carefully, dreading to see evidence of their use in the traditional way. Outside there, on the telegraph wire, sat one of the birds, very much at home; it was the height of the season, and the country was swarming with young birds. Now, if ever, they should lay up for the future, and prove their right to the name, or kill to amuse themselves, if that were their object. But the closest scrutiny failed to reveal one thorn that was, or, so far as I could see, ever had been, used for any purpose whatever. There was not another spiny tree in the vicinity, and I came away relieved.

One more interview I was happy enough to have with my little gray friends. Coming leisurely along on my way home from the glen one noon, I saw two of them sitting on the wire of a fence beside the road. I had never been so near them, and stopped instantly to have a close look, and perhaps settle the question whether the black band on the side of the head ended at the beak, or crossed over the forehead and met its fellow. I found, at this short range, that the light part of the plumage was covered with fine but decided wavy bars, which gave it an exquisite look, and proved the bird to be the great northern, rather than the loggerhead shrike (I couldn't bear to have my bright beauty called a loggerhead).

Very gradually I drew nearer, till I was not more than six feet from them, and could see them clearly, while they remained perfectly self-possessed for ten or fifteen minutes that I stood there. So near was I that I could see the white eyelids, and the tiny feet, which seemed hardly strong enough to hold them on their perch, and explained their preference for wires to rest on.

FEATHERS OR FUR?

One of the little fellows had his back to me, showing the beautiful white markings on his wings as they lie closed and folded together. Near the end of them were white lines making on the black feathers a figure resembling what is known in needlework as a "crow's-foot," perhaps an inch in width, and, a little above this, two dainty waved bars met like a pair of eye-brows. The marking was elegant in the extreme.

While I looked, the bird nearest me suddenly lost what little interest he had in my doings, turned his eyes downward, and in a moment dropped upon a big grasshopper, which he carried in his beak to a wire near the ground to dispose of. Evidently, however, he was not quite ready to eat, for he deliberately lifted one foot, took the grasshopper in his claw, and instantly ejected upon the ground a dark-colored bolus, I should judge half an inch in diameter, and more than twice as long. Then he returned to his grasshopper and made short work of it.

This seemed only to sharpen his appetite, for in a moment he dragged out from the grass something which startled me. Was it feathers or fur or a bit of old rag?

I could soon tell, for he was not in the least ashamed or secretive about it. He pulled it to where a fallen wire lay very near the ground, threw it partly over the wire, plainly as a hold to pull against, and then jerked off a mouthful, which he ate. Again and again did he fling it over the wire, for it soon slipped off, and it was perfectly plain that the object was to give him purchase to pull against. Then I could see small legs on the fragment, and a tail like a mouse's. While I stood watching this feast in progress, a call came from across the road. It was not loud, and it was of a quality hard to express, not exactly harsh, nor yet musical. It was instantly answered by the two on the fence, and the one I was watching dropped his fresh meat and joined his parent. Then I examined the remains of his meat, and found that it had reddish brown fur, a tail not so long but resembling that of a mouse. It was on the borders of a recently cut field of wheat, and it was doubtless some species of ground mouse, a common field mouse, I have reason to believe.

And that was the last I saw of the pretty gray birds that year.

III.

A THORN-TREE NEST.

June was drawing to a close; hermit thrushes and veeries had turned their energies to seeking food for hungry young mouths; rose-breasted grosbeaks and golden orioles, as well as their more humbly clad fellow-creatures, were passing their days near the ground, in the same absorbing work; tree-tops were deserted, and singing was nearly over.

It was well, then, that I should leave my beloved woods, and betake myself to a barren country road, where, in a lonely thorn-tree, a bird of another sort than these had set up late housekeeping, a shrike.

The reputation of this bird of solitary tastes is not attractive. He is quarrelsome and unfriendly with his kind, and aggressive and malicious toward others, says the Oracle. His pleasure is to torture and destroy; no sweet or tender sentiment may cling about his life; in fact, he is altogether unlovely. So declare the books, and so, with additions and exaggerations, says nearly every one who takes birds for his theme. He is branded everywhere as the "butcher-bird," and it seems to be the aim of each writer to discover in his conduct something a little more sanguinary, a shade more depraved, than any predecessor has done.

Now, if the truth is what we are seeking, is it not desirable to see for ourselves, or, as Emerson puts it, "leave others' eyes, and bring your own"? If one can give to the task patient observation, with a loving spirit, a desire to interpret faithfully and to see the best instead of the worst, may he not perchance find that the bird is not the monster he is pictured? And though the story be not so sensational, is it not better to clear up than to blacken the reputation of a fellow-creature, even a very small one in feathers?

This thing it had long been in my heart to do,—to see with my own eyes what enormities the beautiful butcher-bird is guilty of. I left hermits and veeries, I said adieu to sandpipers and grosbeaks, and went to the village to abide with the shrike family. No more delightful mornings in the blessed woods; no more long, dreamy twilights filled with the music of thrushes and the singing brook; no more charming views of the near Green Mountains, gray in the morning light, glorious rosy purple under the setting sun; no more solitary communion with helpful and healing nature. My household gods must now be set up among people, with their cares and troubles, where the immense tragedy of human life is constantly forced into notice; and in no place in the wide world is there more tragedy in every-day life than in peaceful and pious New England.

Change of residence was not so simple an affair with me as it is with the birds; would that it were! I had to spend half a day packing, and another half undoing the work. I had to secure another temporary home, where certain conveniences to which we human beings are slaves should not be lacking, and with a family one could endure under the same roof. All this must needs be settled before I could call on my new neighbors. Time and patience accomplished everything, although the mercury was soaring aloft among the nineties all the time; and at last came the morning when I seated myself before the household I proposed to interview for the benefit of the readers of our day, who demand (say the newspaper authorities) facts and details of daily lives that were of old considered private matters.

On these lines, therefore, I proceeded to study my shrikes. What I discovered by watching early and late, by peeping at them before breakfast and spying upon them after supper,—what they eat and drink, how they behave to one another and their neighbors, what they have to say or to sing, in fact, their whole story so far as it was revealed to me,—I shall set down, nothing extenuating. Other observers may have seen very different things, but that only proves what I am constantly asserting: that birds are individuals; that because one shrike does a certain thing is no sign that another will do the same; it is not safe to judge the species *en masse*. This, therefore, is the true chronicle of what I saw of one pair of loggerhead shrikes (*Lanius ludovicianus*), in the northern extremity of Vermont, about the first of July, 1894.

The discovery of the nest in the thorn-tree was not my own. A friend and fellow bird-lover, driving one evening up this road, startled a bird from the nest, and, checking her horse, looked on in amazement while, one after another, six full-grown shrikes emerged from the tree and flew away. Pondering this strange circumstance she drove on, and when returning looked sharply out for the thorn-tree. This time one bird flew from the nest, which seemed to settle the question of ownership. The next day and the next this experience was repeated, and then the news was brought to me in the woods.

It was a lonely road, leading to nothing except a pasture and a distant farm or two, and the presence of a member of the human race was almost as rare as it was in the forest itself. On one side stretched a pasture with high rail fence; on the other, a meadow guarded by barbed wire. A traveler over this uninviting way soon left the last house in the village behind, and then the only human dwellings in sight were some deserted farm buildings on a hill a mile or more away. Not a tree offered grateful shade, and not a bush relieved the bare monotony of this No Thoroughfare.

But it had its full share of feathered residents. Just beyond the last house, a wren, bubbling over with joy, always poured out his enchanting little song as I passed. Under the deep grass of the meadow dwelt bobolinks and meadow larks; from the pasture rose the silver threadlike song of the savanna sparrow and the martial note of the kingbird. Occasionally I had a call from a family of flickers, or golden-wings, from the woods beyond the pasture; the four young ones naïve and imperative in their manners, bowing vehemently, with emphatic "peauk" that seemed to demand the reason of my presence in their world; while the more experienced elders uttered their low "ka-ka-ka," whether of warning to the young or of pride in their spirit one could only guess. A hard-working oriole papa, with a peremptory youngster in tow, now and then appeared in the pasture; and swallows, both barn and eave, came in merry, chattering flocks from their homes at the edge of the village.

About the middle of the long stretch of road was a solitary maple-tree, and about thirty feet from it, and just within the pasture fence, the thorn, and the nest of my hopes. Approaching quietly on that first morning, I unfolded my camp-chair and sat down in the shade of the maple. The thorn-tree before me was perhaps fifteen feet high. It divided near the ground into two branches, which drew apart, bent over, and became nearly horizontal at their extremities. On one of these main stems, near the end, where it was not more than an inch and a half in diameter, with neither cross-branch nor twig to make it secure, was placed the nest. It was a large structure, at least twice the size of a robin's nest, made apparently of coarse twigs and roots, with what looked like bits of turf or moss showing through the sides, and why it did not fall off in the first strong wind was a mystery. Parallel with the limb on which it rested, and only a few inches above it, was another branch, that must, one would think, be seriously in the way of the coming and going, the feeding and care-taking, inseparable from life in the nest.

THE NEST IN VIEW.

From my post of observation, the thorn-tree was silhouetted against the sky, for it stood on the edge of a slight descent. Every twig and leaf was distinctly visible, while the openings in the foliage were so numerous that not a wing could flit by without my seeing it. The nest itself was partially veiled by a bunch of leaves. What the view might be from the other side I did not investigate that morning; I preferred to leave the birds the slight screen afforded by the foliage, for since there could be no pretense of hiding myself from them, my desire was to let them fancy themselves hidden from me, and

27

so feel free from constraint and be natural in their actions. I hoped, by approaching quietly and unobtrusively, by being careful never to frighten or disturb them in any way, to convince them that I was harmless, and to induce them to forget, or at least ignore, my silent presence. And it seemed possible that I might be gratified, for I had been seated but a few minutes when a shrike flew up from the ground and entered the nest, and, I was pleased to see, with no apparent concern about me.

For the next three hours I took my eyes off the nest only to follow the movements of the owners thereof; and I learned that sitting had begun, and that the brooding bird was fed by her mate. He came, always from a distance, directly to the nest, alighted on the edge, leaned over and gave one poke downward, while low yearning or pleading cries reached my ears. Without lingering an instant he flew to a perch a foot above, stood there half a minute, and then went to the ground. Not more than thirty seconds elapsed before he returned to his mate, the cries greeted him, the mouthful was administered, and he took his leave in exactly the same way as before. He was a personage of methodical habits. This little performance of seeking food on the ground and carrying it to his partner on the nest was repeated five or six times in close succession, and then he rose higher than his tree and took flight for a distant hill, looking, as he flew, like a fluttering bit of black-and-white patchwork. On further acquaintance, I found this to be the regular habit of the bird: to come to his nest and feed his mate thoroughly, and then to take himself away for about half an hour, though later he fell to lingering and watching me.

Left thus alone and well fed, madam was quiet for some time, perhaps ten minutes, and then she went out for exercise or for lunch; flying directly to the ground near the tree, and returning in a few minutes to her place.

FEEDING HIS MATE.

On one occasion I saw what sort of food the shrike collected. He had alighted on the wire fence, apparently to inquire into my business, when his eyes fell upon something desirable—from his point of view. Instantly he dropped to the road, picked up a black object, worm or beetle, an inch long, and took it at once to his mate. Sometimes he carried his prey to a post, and beat it a while before presenting it to her; and one evening, somewhat later than usual, he was found industriously gleaning food from the hosts of the air, flying up in the manner of a flycatcher, and to all appearance with perfect success.

The loggerhead shrike is one of our most beautiful birds, clear blue-gray above, and snowy white below. His black wings are elegantly marked with white, and his black tail, when spread like a fan, as he wheels to alight, showing broad tips and outer feathers of white, is one of his most striking marks. He is a little smaller than a robin, and his mate is of the same size, and as finely dressed as he. The resemblance he is said to bear to the mockingbird I have never been able to see. His form, his size, his coloring, and his movements are, to my sight, in every way different from those of the southern bird.

The manners of the shrike are as fine as one would expect from so distinguished-looking a personage, dignified, reposeful, and unusually silent. I have seen him, once or twice, flirt his half-opened tail and jerk his wings, but he rarely showed even so much impatience or restlessness. He sat on the fence and regarded me, or he drove away an intrusive neighbor, with the same calm and serious air with which he did everything. I have heard of pranks and fantastic performances, of strange, uncouth, and absurd cries, and of course it is impossible to say what vagaries he might have indulged in if he had thought himself unobserved, but in many hours and days of close study of this bird I saw nothing of the kind. The only utterance I heard from him, excepting his song, of which I shall speak presently, was a rattling cry with which he pursued an intruder, and a soft, coaxing "yeap" when he came to the nest and found his mate absent.

One of the most prominent traits of this bird, as we find him depicted in the books and the popular writings, is his quarrelsome and cruel disposition; and "brigand," "assassin," "murderer," and "butcher" are names commonly applied to him.

FRIENDLY RELATIONS.

I watched the shrike several hours daily for weeks, and from the first I was every moment on the alert for the slightest manifestation of these characteristics; and what did I find out? First as to his quarrelsome disposition, his unfriendliness with his own species. I have already spoken of the amicable association, in the very nesting-tree, of half a dozen of the birds, as reported by a trustworthy and experienced observer. On one occasion, somewhat later, I saw an exhibition of a similar friendliness among four adult shrikes. They were frolicking about another thorn-tree in the same pasture, in the most peaceful manner; and while I looked, one of them picked up a tidbit from the ground and flew to the nest I was watching, thus proving that the nesting-bird was one of the group. At least twice afterward, when silently approaching the nest, I found two other shrikes hopping about with the one I was studying, on the ground, almost under the tree. On my appearance the strangers flew, and the nest-owner went up to his mate with an offering. We do not think of calling the robin or bluebird particularly quarrelsome, yet fancy one of these birds allowing another of his species to come to his home-tree! Every close observer of bird-ways knows that it is apparently the first article in the avian creed to keep every other bird away from the nest.

And how did the terrible "brigand" treat his neighbors? The robin, indeed, he drove away, but meadow larks sang and "sputtered" at their pleasure, not only beside him on the fence, but on his own small tree; goldfinches flew over, singing and calling, and no notice was taken of them; sparrows hopped about among the branches of the thorn at their discretion; a chickadee one day made searching examination of nearly every twig and leaf, going close to and over the nest, where the sitting bird must have seen him, yet not a peep arose. Sometimes, when madam left her nest for refreshment, she would sweep by a bird who happened to be on the tree, thus making him fly, but she never followed or showed any special interest in him. Whatever other shrikes may be or do, at least this pair, and the three or four others who visited them, were amiable with their neighbors, small as well as great.

If bravery is a virtue,—and why is it not, in feathers as well as in broadcloth? —the shrike should stand high in our estimation, for he does not hesitate to attack and make his prey animals which few birds of his size dare touch; not only mice, but creatures as well armed as gophers and others.

I was particularly desirous to hear the song of the shrike. He is not classed with singing birds, and is not, I think, usually credited with being musical. But Thoreau speaks of his song, and others mention it. John Burroughs tells of a shrike singing in his vicinity in winter, "a crude broken warble,"— "saluting the sun as a robin might have done." Winter, indeed, seems to be his chosen time for singing, and an ornithologist in St. Albans says that in that season he sings by the hour in the streets of the town.

Therefore did I sit unobtrusively on the near side of the thorn-tree, leaving the birds their screen, to encourage them to sing; and at last I had my reward. One very hot day I did not reach my place under the maple till after nine o'clock, and I found the shrike, as I frequently did, on the fence, on guard. In a few moments, when I had become quiet, he went to the nest, and sitting there on the edge, hidden from my distinct view, he condescended to sing, a low, sweet song, truly musical, though simple in construction, being merely a single clear note followed by a trill several tones higher. After delivering this attractive little aria a dozen or more times, he flew out of the tree and over my head, and sang no more.

My curiosity about his song being thus gratified, I decided to seek a better post of observation; for I hoped every day to find that sitting was over, and the young had appeared. I therefore walked farther up the road, quite past the tree, and took my seat beside the fence, where I could see the whole nest perfectly. The birds at once recognized that all hope of concealment was over, and became much more wary. The singer came less frequently, and was received in silence. Also he took me under strict surveillance, perching on a dead branch of the maple-tree, and sitting there half an hour at a time, motionless but wide awake; ready, no doubt, to defend the nest if I made hostile demonstrations toward it.

For a long time I had my lonely road to myself, almost the sole passer-by being a boy who drove the village cows back and forth, and whom I had taken pains to interest in the safety of the little family. But such a state of things could not last. One morning, as I sat in my usual place, I noticed a party of girls starting out with baskets and pails after berries. They scattered over the meadow, and while I trembled for meadow lark and bobolink babies, I hoped they would not see me; but one of them came directly to the thorn-tree. As she approached, I turned away, as if I had no particular interest in the tree, but, unfortunately, just as she was passing, the bird flew off the nest. The girl looked up, and instantly shouted to me, "Oh, here's a bird's-nest!" "Yes," I replied, knowing that my best policy was to claim it, "that's the nest I am watching." After a sharp look at the tree she went on; but I was much disturbed, for I regard a nest discovered almost the same as a nest robbed. Would she tell? Should I some day find the nest broken up or destroyed? Every morning, after that, I took my long, lonely walk with misgivings, and did not feel easy till I had seen the birds.

SEARCHING THE THORNS.

One very notorious habit of the shrike I had been especially desirous of investigating—that of impaling his prey. Judging from what has been written about him, it must be a common performance, his daily business, and I confidently expected to see his thorn-tree adorned, from roots to topmost twig, with grasshoppers and beetles, not to mention small birds and animals. Early in my visits to him, I looked the tree over carefully, and, not content with my own eyes, called in the aid of a friend. Moreover, we together made diligent search in the only other thorn-tree in the vicinity, one spoken of above. Not a sign could we discover in either tree of any such use of a thorn, though thorns were there in abundance.

Again, one day I saw the bird very busy about the barbed-wire fence, and remembering to have seen the statement that shrikes in the West, where thorn-trees are absent, impale their grasshoppers on the barbs, I thought, "Now I have surely caught you at it!" I did not disturb him, and he worked at that spot some time. But when he had gone I hastened over to see what beetle or bird he had laid up, when behold, the barbs were as empty as the thorns. In fact, I was never able to find the smallest evidence that the bird ever does impale anything, and the St. Albans ornithologist spoken of adds as his testimony that he has often examined the haunts of this bird, but has never found anything impaled. And a correspondent in Vermont writes me that he watched the shrike for twenty years, on purpose to see this performance, and in all that time saw but three instances, one being a field mouse, and the other two English sparrows.

All this, of course, does not prove that the shrike never impales his prey, but it does prove that he does not spend all his time at the work; and while I have no doubt he has the habit, I believe the accounts of it are very much exaggerated.

On the morning of the Fourth of July, a cool, and in that remote part of the world a delightfully quiet day, I felt an unaccountable disinclination to make my usual visit to the shrikes. Refusing, however, to yield to that feeling, I forced myself to take the long walk, and seat myself in my usual place. But I could not feel much surprise when, after more than an hour's close watching, the birds failed to appear, and I became convinced that they were gone. Whether shot by man or boy, robbed by beast or bird or human, it was plain I had seen the last of the thorn-tree family; for I knew positively that in that hour no one had gone to or come from the nest, and I was sure, from my knowledge of her, that the sitting bird would not remain an hour without eating, even if her mate had stayed away so long. Of course, I concluded, that girl had told her discovery, and some boy had heard, and broken up the home. I looked carefully on every side. The nest seemed undisturbed, but not a sign of life appeared about it, and sadly enough I folded my chair and went back to the village.

"PAUPERIZING" A BIRD.

Six days passed, in which I avoided going up the lonely road, the scene of my disappointment, but I turned my attention to bird affairs in the town. One case which interested me greatly was of "pauperizing" a bird. It was a least flycatcher, and her undoing was her acceptance of nesting material, which her human friend, the oft-mentioned local bird-lover, supplied. To secure a unique nest for herself, when the flycatcher babies should have abandoned it, this wily personage, who was the accepted providence of half the birds in the vicinity, and on terms of great familiarity with some of them, threw out narrow strips of cloth of various colors, to tempt the small nest-builder. At first the wise little madam refused to use the gayer pieces, but being beguiled by the device of sewing a bright one between two of duller hue, her scruples were overcome; and after that her fall into total dependence was easy and complete. She accepted the most brilliant pieces that were offered, and built her nest therewith.

But alas, from the moment of yielding to her vanity or her love for ease, troubles began in the flycatcher family. The robin nesting in an adjoining tree reproved her by tugging at the gay strings that hung out; the English sparrow across the way set herself up as a conservator of morals, and, to teach Madam Chebek modesty becoming her size, tried to pull the whole to pieces. Then when Chebek, who is no coward, had succeeded in putting an end to neighborly interference, the nest began to show a deplorable disinclination to "stay put." Whether the material could not be properly fastened, or whether the bird was so demoralized as to shirk ordinary precautions, the fact is, that every breeze shook the little structure, and four completed nests of this unnatural sort fell, one after another, in ruins to the ground. Then motherly instinct came to the rescue: she refused further aid, removed herself to a distance, built a new nest, after the accredited flycatcher fashion, and it is supposed brought out her brood safely, if rather late. So hard it is in the bird-world, as in the human, to help, and not hurt.

STRANGE CRIES UP THE ROAD.

More interesting, even, than this flycatcher episode was an adventure one evening when I walked far out on a road, one side of which was deep woods, while the other was bordered by pasture and meadows. My object in going was to hear a white-throated sparrow, who often sang in that vicinity.

I had been resting on my camp-stool very quietly for half an hour, and was just thinking it time to return home, when a strange sort of clacking cry startled me. At first I thought it was made by a frog with a bad cold; but it grew louder, and changed in quality, till it became a whining sound that might be made either by a baby or by some small animal. I looked very carefully up the road whence the sound seemed to come, but saw nothing excepting a robin, who, perched on the highest post of a fence, was looking and listening with great apparent interest, but without making a sound himself,—a very unusual proceeding on the part of this bird, who always has a great deal to say about everything.

The cries increased in volume and frequency, and I started slowly up the road, uncertain whether I should come upon a young fox or other wild beast, but determined to solve the mystery. As I drew near, I began to be conscious of a knocking sound in the woods beside the road. It was like a light tapping on hollow wood, and it regularly followed each cry. I was at once reassured. It must be a woodpecker, I thought,—they make some strange noises, and there was a large one, the pileated, said to inhabit these woods, though I had never been able to see him. I went on more confidently then, for I must see what woodpecker baby could utter such cries. As I continued to advance, though I could still see nothing, I noticed that the tapping grew louder every moment.

Suddenly there was a movement at the edge of a thick clump of ferns, and my eyes fell upon what I thought was, after all, a big toad or frog. It hopped like one of these reptiles, and as it was growing dusky, feathers and fur and bare skin looked much alike. But being anxious to know positively, I went on, and when I reached it I saw that it was a young bird, nearly as big as a robin just out of the nest. Then I dropped all impedimenta, and gave myself unreservedly to the catching of that bird. He fled under the ferns, which were like a thick mat, and I stooped and parted them, he flying ever ahead till he reached the end and came out in sight. Then I pounced upon him, and had him in my hands.

A VOCIFEROUS BABY.

Such a shriek as he gave! while he struggled and bit, and proved himself very savage indeed. More startling, however, than his protest was a cry of anguish that answered it from the woods, a heart-rending, terrible cry, the wail of a mother about to be bereaved. I looked up, and lo! in plain sight, in her agony forgetting her danger, and begging by every art in her power, a cuckoo. Her distress went to my heart; I could not resist her pleading. One instant I held that vociferous cuckoo baby, to have a good look at him, speaking soothingly to the mother the while, and then opened my hand, when he half flew, half scrambled, to the other side of the road, and set up another cry, more like that of his mother. Seeing her infant at liberty, she slipped back into the woods and resumed the calls, which sounded so remarkably like tapping, while he started up the road, answering; and thus I left them.

Several times after that, I heard from the woods—for

"The cuckoo delights in the cool leafy shadows

34

Where the nest and its treasures are rocked by the breeze"—

the same strange calling of a cuckoo mother, a weird, unearthly, knocking sound, not in the least like the ordinary "kuk! kuk!" of the bird. I should never have suspected that it was anything but the tap of an unusually cautious woodpecker, if I had not caught her at it that night.

On the sixth evening after I had thought myself bereaved of the shrikes, I went out for a walk with my friend, and we turned our steps into the lonely road. As we approached the thorn, what was my surprise to see the shrike in his old place on the fence, and, after waiting a few minutes, to see his mate go to the ground for her lunch, as if nothing had happened!

Then they had not deserted! But how and why all life about the nest had been suspended for one hour on the Fourth of July is a puzzle to this day. However it may have happened, I was delighted to find the birds safe, and at once resumed my study; going out the next morning as usual, staying some hours, and again toward night for another visit.

Now I was sure it must be time for the young to be out, for I knew positively that the bird had been sitting fourteen days, and twenty-one days had passed since she was frightened off her nest twice in one day.

I redoubled my vigilance, but I saw no change in the manners of the pair till the morning of July 12th. All night there had been a heavy downpour, and the morning broke dismally, with strong wind and a drizzling rain. I knew the lonely road would be most unattractive, but no vagaries of wind or weather could keep me away at this crisis. I found it all that I had anticipated—and more. The clay soil was cut up from fence to fence by cows' feet, and whether it presented an unbroken puddle or a succession of small ones made by the hoof-prints, it was everywhere so slippery that retaining one's footing was no slight task, and of course there was no pretense of a sidewalk. Add to this the difficulty of holding an umbrella against the fierce gusts, and it may be imagined that my pathway that morning was not "strewn with roses."

STUDY UNDER DIFFICULTIES.

In some fashion, however, I did at last reach the thorn-tree, planted my chair in the least wet spot I could find, and, tucking my garments up from the ground, sat down. At first I discarded my unmanageable umbrella, till the raindrops obscuring my opera-glass forced me to open it again. And all these preliminaries had to be settled before I could so much as look at the nest.

Something had happened, as I saw at once; the manners of the birds were very different from what they had been all these days I had been studying them. Both of them were at the nest when I looked, but in a moment one flew, and the other slipped into her old seat, though not so entirely into it as usual.

Heretofore she had been able to hide herself so completely that it was impossible to tell whether she were there or not. Even the tail, which in most birds is the unconcealable banner that proclaims to the bird-student that the sitter is at home, even this unruly member she had been able to hide in some way, but this morning it remained visible.

In a minute the shrike returned and fed somebody,—I suppose his mate, since she did not move aside; and again in another minute he repeated the operation. So he went on bringing food perhaps a dozen times in close succession. Then he rested a few minutes, when she who through the long days of sitting had been so calm and quiet seemed all at once as restless as any warbler. She rose on the edge of the nest, and uttered the low, yearning cry I had heard from him, then flew to the ground, returned, perched on the edge, leaned over, and gave three pokes as if feeding. Then she flew to another part of the tree, thence to a fence post, then back again to the edge of the nest. In a moment the uneasy bird slipped into her old place, but, apparently too restless to stay, was out again in a few seconds, when she stood up in the nest and began calling,—a loud but musical two-note call, the second tone a third higher than the first, and different from anything I had heard from her before. If it were a call to her mate, he did not at once appear, and she relieved her feelings by flying to the maple and perching a few minutes, though so great was the attraction at home that she could stay away but a short time.

LOVELY, INNOCENT YOUNGLINGS.

Of course I concluded from all this that the young shrikes were out, and I longed with all my heart to stay and watch the charming process of changing from the ungainly creatures they were at that moment to the full-grown and feathered beauties they would be when they appeared on the tree; to see them getting their education, learning to follow their parents about, and finally seeking their own food, still keeping together in a family party, as I had seen them once before, elsewhere,—lovely, innocent younglings whom surely no one could find it in his heart to call "butchers" or "assassins." Then, too, I wanted to see the head of the family, who in the character of spouse had shown himself so devoted, so above reproach, in the new rôle of father and teacher, in which I had no doubt he would be equally admirable.

But dearly as I love birds, there are other ties still dearer, and just then there came a call that made me leave the pair with their new joy, pack my trunks, and speed, night and day, half way across the continent, beyond the Great Divide, to a certain cozy valley in the heart of the Rocky Mountains.

Before I left, however, I committed the little family in the thorn-tree to the care of my friend the bird-lover; and a few weeks later there came over the mountains to me this conclusion to the story, written by Mrs. Nelly Hart Woodworth, of St. Albans:—

"I was at the shrikes' nest Thursday last. I sat down on the knoll beyond the nest, and waited quietly for fifteen minutes. No signs of life in nest or neighborhood, save the yearning cry of the lark, as it alighted on the top of the thorn-tree. After I was convinced that, in some unaccountable manner, the shrikes had been spirited away before they were half big enough, I changed my place to the other side of the tree, out of sight from the nest. When I had been there for a long time, I heard distinctly a low whispering in the nest, and lo! the butcher babies had become sentient beings, and were talking very softly and sweetly among themselves. They had evidently miscalculated about my departure. Then two or three little heads stuck out above the edge, and the soft stirring of baby wings was apparent. They cuddled and nestled and turned themselves, and one little butcher hoisted himself upon the upper side of the nest, stood upright briefly and beat his wings, then sank into the nest, which was full of life and movement. So much for that day.

"Friday one stood upon the edge of the nest, and others looked out, but no feeding bird came.

SHAKEN OUT OF THE NEST.

"Saturday I was in fortune, as I met in the vicinity the boy who drives the village cows. Two heads only were visible over the edge. But the boy, with a boy's genius for investigation, brought a fence rail, put it under the branch, and shook them up a little. They only huddled closer. At my suggestion he gave a more vigorous shake, and a baby climbed from the nest, a foot or two above, then flew as well as anybody clear lip into the top of the tree. Such a pretty baby! breast white as snow, lovely black crescent through the eyes, and the dearest little tail imaginable, half an inch long, and flirted up and down continually.

"The other bird—for there were but two—ran up the twigs for two feet, but quickly returned to the nest, and would not leave it again, though we could see its wondering eyes look out and peer at us. Both were gone the next day (twelve days old). And thus endeth the butcher episode."

Now also must end—for a time—my study of this interesting bird. But I shall not forget it, and I shall seek occasion to study it again and again, till I have proved, if I find it true, that the shrike deserves better of us than the character we have given him; that he is not nearly "so black as he is painted."

IV.

THE WITCHING WREN.

"There is madness about thee, and joy divine
　　In that song of thine."

The song of the winter wren is something that must be heard to be appreciated; words can no more describe it than they can paint the sky at evening, or translate the babble of the mountain brook.

"Canst thou copy in verse one chime
Of the wood bird's peal and cry?"

This witching carol, one of nature's most alluring bits of music, fell upon my ear for the first time one memorable morning in June. It was a true siren-strain. We forgot, my comrade and I, what we were seeking in the woods. The junco family, in their snug cave among the roots, so interesting to us but now, might all fly away; the oven-bird, in the little hollow beside the path, might finish her lace-lined domicile, and the shy tanager conclude to occupy the nest on the living arch from which we had frightened her,—all without our being there to see. For the moment we cared for but one thing,—to follow that "wandering voice," to see that singer.

THE DOG BECOMES INTERESTED.

Silently we arose, folded our camp-stools, and started. We wished to move without sound; but the woods were dry, and every dead stick snapped with a crack; every fallen leaf rustled with a startling sound; every squirrel under whose tree we chanced to pass first shrieked, and then subsided into a sobbing cry or a scolding bark, according as his fur was gray or red. A procession of elephants could hardly make more noise, or create more consternation among the residents of the forest, than we three (counting the dog), when we wished to be silent as shadows. But the wren sang on. Evidently, he was accustomed to squirrel vagaries, and snapping twigs did not disturb him. Nearer and nearer sounded the song, and more and more enraptured we became. We were settling ourselves to listen and to look for our charmer, when the third member of our party created a diversion. Wrens had no attraction for him, but he came upon the scent of something he was interested in, and instantly fell to pawing the ground and tearing up the obstructing roots with his teeth, as though he had gone suddenly mad.

The door through which had doubtless vanished some delectable mouse or mole was, when discovered, of a proper size for his small body, but in less than a minute it was big enough to admit the enormous head of the dog, who varied his eager tearing up of the soil with burying his head and shoulders in the hole he had made; smelling and listening a few seconds, then jerking it out with a great snort, and devoting himself with fresh vigor to digging. It was a curious contrast to the indifference with which he usually accompanied us, but it proved that he had his enthusiasms, if he did not share ours. We could not but be amused, notwithstanding the delicious trilling notes that drew us grew fainter and fainter, and we despaired of seeing our songster till the important affairs of that mouse should be settled. Arguments were of no avail with the four-footed sportsman, a rival attraction failed to attract, and commands were thrown away on him in his excited state. We were forced to go home without the sight we desired.

We were not the first to be fascinated by this marvelous melody. "Dull indeed must be the ear that thrills not on hearing it," says Audubon, and its effect upon him is worth telling. He was traveling through a swamp, where he had reason to suspect the presence of venomous snakes and other reptiles. While moving with great circumspection, looking out for these unwelcome neighbors, the captivating little aria burst upon his ear. Instantly snakes were forgotten, his absorbing passion took full possession, and he crashed recklessly through the briers and laurels in pursuit. It is pleasant to know, further, that he found not only the singer, but his nest, which was the first he had ever seen, and gave him a delight known only to enthusiastic bird-lovers.

FOREST SOUNDS.

The morning after the absurd incident of a mouse-hunt, by the dog who in his character of protector was our daily companion, we started out afresh, with ears for nothing but wren songs. Making a wide détour to avoid the scene of yesterday's excitement, we were soon comfortably seated near the spot the wren seemed to haunt, and silence fell between us. That is to say, *we* were quiet, though nothing is farther from the truth than our common expression "silent woods." The forest is never silent. Hushed it may be of man's clamor, and empty as well of his presence, but it is filled with sounds from its own abundant life; not so loud, perhaps, and aggressive to the ear as the rumble of Broadway, but fully as continuous; and if the human wanderer in its delightsome shades will but bring his own noisy progress to a halt, he will enjoy a new sensation. There is the breeze that sets all the leaves to whispering, not to speak of rougher winds that fill the dim aisles with a roar like Niagara. There are the falling of dead twigs, the rustle of leaves under the footsteps of some small shy creature in fur, the dropping of nuts, and the tapping of woodpeckers. There are the voices of the wood-dwellers,—not songs alone, but calls and utterances of many kinds from birds; cries and scolding of squirrels, who have a *répertoire* astonishing to those who do not know them; squawks and squeals of little animals more often heard than seen; and, not least, the battle-cries of the winged hosts "who come with songs to greet you" wherever and whenever you may appear.

Moreover, the moment one of the human race is quiet,—such is our reputation for unrest,—the birds grow suspicious, and take pains to announce to all whom it may concern that here is an interloper in nature. Even if there be present no robin,—vociferous guardian of the peace,—a meek and gentle flicker mounts the highest tree and cries "pe-auk! pe-auk!" as loud as he can shout, a squirrel on one side shrieks at the top of his voice, veeries call anxiously here and there, while a vireo warbles continuously overhead, and a redstart "trills his twittering horn."

When the wren song began, quite near this time, everything else was forgotten, and after a few moments' eager suspense we saw our bird. He was little and inconspicuous in shades of brown, with tail stuck pertly up, wren fashion, foraging among the dead leaves and on old logs, entirely unconscious that he was one of the three distinguished singers of the wood; none but the hermit thrush and the veery being comparable to him. Whenever, in the serious business of getting his breakfast, he reached a particularly inviting twig, or a more than usually nice rest on a log, he threw up his little head and poured out the marvelous strain that had taken us captive, then half hopped, half flew down, with such energy that he "whirred" as he went. We watched his "tricks and manners," and, what was more, we steeped our souls in his music as long as we chose, that morning.

FASCINATED BY A WREN.

The lovely long June days were never more fascinating. Every morning we went into our beloved woods to watch its bird population; to find out who was building, who had already set up housekeeping; to penetrate their secrets, and discover their wonderfully hidden nests. Each day we heard the witching song that never lost its charm for us. One morning—it was the fifteenth of the month—we were sauntering up one of the most inviting paths. The dog was ahead, carrying on his strong and willing neck his mistress's stool, she following closely, steadying the same with her hand, while I, as was my custom, brought up the rear. Suddenly, as we approached a pile of dead limbs from a fallen tree, my friend stopped motionless, and as usual the caravan came to instant halt. Without taking her eyes from the brush heap, she silently pulled the stool from the dog's neck and sat down upon it. I seated myself beside her, and the dog stretched himself at our feet.

"A wren," she whispered briefly, and in a moment I saw it. A mother, no doubt, for her mouth was full of food, and she was fidgeting about on a branch, undecided as yet what she should do, with that formidable array in front of her very door, as it afterward turned out. A wren is a quick-witted little creature, and she was not long in making up her mind. She flitted around us, turned our right flank (so to speak), and vanished behind us.

We took the hint, changed our front, and, after the moment's confusion, subsided again, gently waving our maple boughs to terrorize the foe that was always with us, and keeping sharp watch while we held whispered consultation as to whether that was the winter wren, and the mate of our singer.

"Oh, if she has a nest!" said my comrade, to whose home belonged these woods. "The winter wren is not known to nest here. We must find it."

THE EXCITEMENT OF DISCOVERY.

Silence again, while a tanager called his agitated "chip-chur!" in the tops of the tall beech-trees, a downy woodpecker knocked vigorously at the door of some ill-fated grub in a maple trunk, and the wren burst into his maddest melody afar off. We were not to be lured this morning. We were enjoying the excitement of discoverers. Where a bird is carrying food must be a nest with birdlings, and nothing could draw us from that.

We waited. In a few minutes the bird appeared again with her mate. Was he the singer? Breathless hush on our part, with eyes fixed on the two restless parents, who were anxious to pass us. In a moment one of them became aggressive. He—or she—flew to a twig eight or ten feet from us, jerked himself up in a terrifying way, as though about to annihilate us, and then bowed violently; not intending a polite salutation, as might be supposed, but defiance, threat, or insult. We held our ground, refusing to be frightened away, and at last parental love conquered fear; both of them flew past us at the same instant, went to one spot under the upturned roots of a fallen tree, and in a moment departed together.

My fellow-student hurried eagerly to the place, dropped upon her knees on the wet ground, amid rank ferns and weeds, leaned far under the overhanging roots with their load of black earth, thrust careful fingers into something, and then rose, flushed and triumphant.

"Come here," she commanded. "A nest full of babies! Oh, what luck!"

There it was, sure enough, away back under the heavy roof of earth and roots, a snug round structure of green moss, little bigger than a croquet ball. The hole occupied by the roots when the tree stood erect was now filled with water, and before it waved a small forest of ferns. It was an ideal situation for a nest; pleasant to look at, and safe—if anything could be safe—from the small fur-clad gentry who claimed the wood and all it contained for their own.

41

> "The hermit has no finer eye
>   For shadowy quietness"

than had this pair of wise little wrens.

From the blissful moment of our discovery, whatever interesting excursion was planned, whatever choice nest to be sought, or charming family of nestlings to be called upon, our steps first turned of themselves up the wren path. Every day we saw the birds go in and out, on household cares intent, and we soon began to look for the exit of the younglings.

I WAS STARTLED.

During this time of close watching, it happened that for a day or two I was obliged to make my visit alone. Why is it that solitude in the depths of the forest has so mysterious an effect on the imagination? One dreads to make a noise, and though having nothing to fear, he instinctively steals about as if every tree concealed a foe. The first morning I sauntered along the lonely paths in silence, admiring for the hundredth time the trunks of the trees, with their varied decorations of lichen and their stately moss-grown insteps, and pausing a moment before the butternut which had divided itself in early youth, and now supported upon one root three tall and far-spreading trees. I had not heard the wren; and indeed the birds seemed unusually silent, the squirrels appeared to be asleep in their nests, and not a leaf was stirring. Wordsworth's admonition came into my mind:—

> "Move along these shades
> In gentleness of heart; with gentle hand
> Touch—for there is a spirit in the woods."

Suddenly something sprang out from under a tree, as I passed, jerked at my gown, and ran after with noisy footsteps. I started, and quickly turned to face my assailant, expecting to see a bear at least. I found instead—a dead branch which had caught in my dress and was dragging behind me. I loosened the branch from its hold, and went on. But though I laughed at the absurdity, I found my nerves a little shaken. Just as I reached the wren corner a shriek arose, as if I had stepped on a whole family of birdlings. Again I started, when a saucy squirrel ran out on the branch of a tree, scolding me in good round terms.

It is impossible to discourage or tire out a squirrel; his business is never pressing, and if it were he considers it an important part of his duties to see that no one interferes with the nests he depends on for fresh eggs. He is sure to keep up a chatter which puts all the birds of the neighborhood on their guard; and as I was particularly desirous not to reveal to him the position of the wrens' nest, I stayed only long enough to assure myself that the little birds

42

had not flown, and the parents were attending strictly to domestic affairs.

The next day I succeeded in reaching the wren quarter without arousing the ire of the squirrels, and I placed my seat very near the nest to see if the bird had learned not to fear me. Fixing my eyes on the place she must enter, I waited, motionless. Some time passed, and though I heard many bird notes about me, and the wren song itself afar off, there was no flit of wing nor faintest wren note near me. But suddenly a shadowy form passed in directly from the front, stayed an instant, and left in the same way. It was perfectly silent, not the slightest rustle of a feather, and it was so near the ground I could not tell whether it flew or ran; it appeared to glide. Brave little creature! I was heartily ashamed of annoying her. I moved my seat to a more respectful distance, and she went in and out as usual.

A BRAVE LITTLE MOTHER.

It was much more satisfactory watching the little mother about her daily cares than trying to keep track of her mate. He was one of the most baffling birds I ever tried to spy upon. Often I heard his delightful song so near that I was sure in a moment I should see him. Then I peered through the low bushes, without moving so much as an eyelash, expecting every instant that my eyes would fall upon him, and certain that not a leaf had rustled nor a twig sprung back, when all at once I heard him on the other side. He had flitted through the underbrush, not flying much, but hopping on or very near the ground, without a breath to betray him. The wren mother could not hide herself so completely from me, there being one spot on earth she could not desert,—the charming nook that held her babies; and yet, be as motionless as I might, I could not deceive her. She never could be convinced that I was a queer-shaped bush, not even when I held a maple bough before my face, and my garments harmonized perfectly with my surroundings. She always came near and bowed to me, jerked herself up, and flirted her wings and tail, as if to say, "I know you. You needn't try to hide." When I went too near, as on the occasion spoken of, while she was much more wary she was not afraid, and I had no compunctions about studying her quaint ways.

We were exceedingly desirous of seeing that family start out in life, and we did, in a way that startled us as much as it must have surprised them. "I wonder if they're gone," was our anxious thought every morning as we approached; and one day, not seeing either parent, we feared they had made their début without our assistance, in the magical morning hours when so many things take place in the bird-world.

"I mean to see if they are still there," said my comrade, creeping up to the mass of roots, leaning far under, and carefully thrusting one finger into the nest.

A dynamite bomb could not have been more effective, nor more shocking to us, for lo! in sudden panic five baby wrens took flight in five different directions. The cause of the disturbance rose, with a look of discomfiture on her face, as if she had been caught robbing a nest. She seemed so dismayed that I laughed, while those wrenlings made the air fairly hum about her head.

"ASSISTED" OUT OF THE NEST.

That they were ready to fly, and only waiting for "the Discourager of Hesitancy" to start them, was plain, for every one used his little wings manfully,—perhaps I should say wren-fully,—and flew from fifteen to twenty feet before he came down. In less than a minute the air was filled with wren-baby chirps, and we seated ourselves to await the mother's return and witness the next act in the wren drama. The mother took it philosophically, recognizing the chirps, and locating them with an ease and precision that aroused envy in us bird-lovers, to whom young-bird calls seem to come from every direction at once. She immediately began to feed, and to collect them into a little flock. With her help we also found them, and watched them a long time: their pretty baby ways, their eager interest in the big world, their drawing together as they heard one another's voices, and their cozy cuddling up together on a log.

Feeling that we had made disturbance enough for one day, we finally went home; but the next day, and several days thereafter, we hunted up the little family as it wandered here and there in the woods, noting the putting on of pert wren ways, and the growth of confidence and helpfulness. We identified them fully as the family of our beautiful singer, for we saw him feed them, then mount a projecting root and sing his perfect rhapsody, not fifteen feet from us.

I must explain the name I have used, "the Discourager of Hesitancy." It is the invention of Mr. Frank Stockton, as every one knows, but I applied it to my fellow-student because of her conduct in the case of the wrens; and a day or two later she proved her right to it by her treatment of a chipping-sparrow family near the house. She took hold of the tip end of a branch and drew it down to look at the nest full of young chippies. "They're about ready to fly," she remarked calmly; and at that instant the branch was released, sprang up, and four young birds were suddenly tossed out upon the world. They sailed through the air, too much surprised to use their wings, and dropped back into the tree, which fortunately was a thick evergreen. The "Discourager's" face displayed a mixture of horror and shame that was very droll. She *said* the twig broke, but in the light of her behavior to the wrens, and her avowed pleasure in stirring birds up to see what they would do, I must say I have my suspicions, especially when I remember that that was the second family whose minds she had made up for them that week.

After about ten days of watching the wren family, we lost their lively chirpings, the witching song ceased, the place seemed empty of wren life, and our charming acquaintance with them a thing to be remembered only. At least so we sadly thought, till nearly the end of July, when, on sauntering through the old paths for almost the last time (for me), we heard once more the familiar music, as full, as fresh, as bewitching, as in the spring. We sought the singer, eager to see as well as hear. After a tramp over underbrush and through a swamp, we saw him,—the same delightful bird, so far as we could tell; certainly he had sung the exact song that charmed us in early June. He had probably trained and started out in life his five babies, and now had time as well as inclination to sing again.

During the three days that were left of my stay I heard the enchanting voice every time I went into the woods,

"Chaunting his low impassioned vesper-hymn,
Clear as the silver treble of a stream."

45

V.

WHIMSICAL WAYS IN BIRD-LAND.

"O irritant, iterant, maddening bird!"

One lovely evening in May, I was walking down a quiet road, looking, as usual, for birds, when all at once there burst upon the sweet silence a loud alarm. "Chack! chack! chack! too! too! t-t-t! quawk! quawk!" at the top of somebody's loud resonant voice, as if the whole bird-world had suddenly gone mad. I looked about, expecting to see a general rush to the spot; but, to my surprise, no one seemed to notice it. A catbird on the fence went on with his bewitching song, and a wood thrush in the shrubbery dropped not a note of his heavenly melody.

"They have heard it before; it must be a chat," I said; and lo! on the top twig of a tall tree, brilliant in the setting sun, stood the singer. Never before had I seen one of the family show himself freely; and while I gazed he proceeded to exhibit another phase of chat manners, new to me,—wing antics, of which I had read. He flew out toward another tree-top, going very slowly, with his legs hanging awkwardly straight down. At every beat of the wings he threw them up over his back till they seemed to meet, jerked his expressive tail downward, and uttered a harsh "chack," almost pausing as he did so. "Not only a chat, but a character," was my verdict, as I turned back from my stroll.

AN ECCENTRIC BIRD.

For several years I had been trying to know the most eccentric bird in North America,—the yellow-breasted chat. Two or three times I had been able to study him a little, but never with satisfaction, and I was charmed to discover one of his kind so near the pleasant old family mansion in which I had established myself for the summer. This house, which had been grand in its day, but, like the whole place, was now tottering with age, was an ideal spot for a bird-lover, being delightfully neglected and gone to seed. Berry patches run wild offered fascinating sites for nests; moss-covered apple-trees supplied dead branches for perching; great elms and chestnuts, pines and poplars, scattered over the grounds, untrimmed and untrained, presented something to suit all tastes; and above all, there existed no nice care-taker to disturb the paradise into which Mother Nature had turned it for her darlings.

It was a month later than this before I discovered where the chat and his mate, the image of himself, had taken up their abode for the season, and then I was drawn by his calls to another old tangle of blackberry bramble at the upper edge of the orchard. "Quoik!" he began, very low, and then quickly added, "Whe-up! ch'k! ch'k! toot! toot! too! t-t-t-t-t!" concluding with a very good imitation of a watchman's rattle. I hastened toward the spot, and was again treated to that most absurd wing performance, followed by an exhibition of himself in plain sight, and then a circling around my head, till, tired of pranks or satisfied with his survey, he dropped out of sight in the bushes.

Here, I said to myself, is a chat of an unfamiliar sort; just as eccentric as any of his race, and not at all averse to being seen; wary, but not shy; and at once I was eager to know him, for the great and undying charm of bird study lies in the individuality of these lovely fellow-creatures, and the study of each one is the study of a unique personality, with characteristics, habits, and a song belonging exclusively to itself. Not even in externals are birds counter-parts of one another. Close acquaintance with one differentiates him decidedly from all his fellows; should his plumage resemble that of his brethren,—which it rarely does,—his manners, expressions, attitudes, and specific "ways" are peculiarly his own.

A BLACKBERRY TANGLE.

The blackberry patch pointed out by the chat occupied the whole length of a steep little slope between a meadow and the orchard, and at the lower edge rested against a fence in the last stages of decrepitude. During many years of neglect it had almost returned to a state of wildness. Long, briery runners had bound the whole into an impenetrable mass, forbidding alike to man and beast, and neighboring trees had sprinkled it with a promising crop of seedlings; or, as Lowell pictures it,—

"The tangled blackberry, crossed and recrossed, weaves
A prickly network of ensanguined leaves."

As if planned for the use of birds, at one end stood a delectable watch-tower in the shape of a great elm, and at the other a cluster of smaller trees,—apple, ash, and maple. These advantages had not escaped the keen eyes of our clever little brothers, and it was a centre of busy life during the nesting season.

The first time I attempted to find the chat's nest, the bird himself accompanied me up and down the borders of this well-fortified blackberry thicket, mocking at me, and uttering his characteristic call, a sort of mew, different from that of the catbird or the cat, at the same time carefully keeping his precious body entirely screened by the foliage. Well he knew that no clumsy, garmented human creature however inquisitive, could penetrate his thorny jungle, and doubtless the remarks so glibly poured out were sarcastic or exultant over my failure; for though I walked the whole length, and at every step peered into the bushes, no nest could I discover.

Somewhat later I made the acquaintance of the domestic partner of the chat family. She was less talkative than her spouse, as are most feathered dames—a wise arrangement in the bird-world, for what would become of the nest and nestlings, if the home-keepers had as much to say as their mates? She sat calmly on the fence, as I passed, or dressed her plumage on the branch of a tree, uttering no sound except, rarely, the common mewing call. She was a wise little thing, too. When I caught her carrying a locust, and at once concluded she had young to feed, as quickly as if she had read my thoughts she let her prey drop, looking at me, as who should say, "You see I am not carrying food." But though I admired her quick wit and respected her motive, I did not believe the little mother, and despite the attractiveness of the head of the household I kept close watch upon her, hoping to track her home. I soon observed that she always rose from the tangle at one spot near the elm; but vainly did I creep through what once might have been a path between the blackberries, though I did have the satisfaction of seeing the singer uneasy, and of feeling sure that, as the children say, I was "very warm."

A CUNNING DAME.

Day after day, in fair weather or foul, in cold or heat, I took my way down the lane, and seated myself as comfortably as circumstances would admit, to spy upon the brown-and-gold family; and day after day I was watched in turn,—sometimes by the singer, restlessly flying from tree to tree, peering down to study me from all sides, and amusing me with all his varied eccentricities of movement and song, if one may thus name his vocal performances. Occasionally madam condescended to entertain, or, what is more probable, tried to perplex me by her tactics. She scorned the transparent device of drawing me away from the dangerous vicinity by pretending to be hurt, or by grotesque exhibitions. Her plan was far more cunning than these: it was to point out to the eager seeker after forbidden knowledge, convenient places where the nest might be—but certainly was not,—and so to bewilder the spy, by many hints, that she would not realize it when the real passage to the waiting nestlings was made. The wise little matron would alight on the fence and look anxiously down, seemingly about to drop into the nest; then, as if she really could not make up her mind to do so while I looked on, fly to a blackberry spray and do it all over again. In a moment she would repeat the performance from an elm sapling, and again turn anxious and lingering glances in still another direction. Then, as if now she surely must go home, she would slip in among the bushes, apparently trying to keep out of sight. At last, having thoroughly mystified me, and confused my ideas past clearing up, with a dozen or more hints, she would fly over the small elm and disappear, in a different direction from any one of the places she had with such pretended reluctance pointed out. Nor was the nest to be found by following any of her hints.

One day, when the beguiling little dame had exasperated me beyond endurance, I suddenly resolved to track her to the nest, if it took the whole day. So when she flung herself, in her usual way, over the small elm, I instantly followed, in my humbler fashion. Under the fence I crept, through the patched-up opening the cows had broken through, and up the path they had attempted to make. Now I fully appreciated the wisdom of the bird in the choice of a nesting-site. The very blackberry bushes appeared to league themselves together for her protection, stretching long, detaining arms, and clutching my garments in all sorts of unexpected and impossible ways; and while I carefully disengaged one, half a dozen others snatched at me in new quarters, till, in despair, I jerked away, leaving a portion of my gown in their grasp. Thus fighting my way, inch by inch, I progressed slowly, until the chat's becoming silent encouraged me to fling prudence to the winds, and pull aside every bush at the risk of tearing the flesh off my hands on the briers.

A NEST AT LAST!

At last a nest! My heart beat high. I struggled nearer, cautiously, not to alarm the owner; for though I must see the nest, I had no desire to disturb it. I parted the vines and looked in. Empty, and plainly a year old!

Forgetting the brambles in my disappointment, I turned hastily away, when the bush, as if in revenge for my discovery of its secret, seized my garments in a dozen places; and suffering in gown and temper, I tore myself away from the birds' too zealous guardians and wandered up the lane.

The lane was an enticing spot, with young blackberry runners stretching out tender green bloom toward whom they might reach, and clematis rioting over and binding together in flowery chains all the shrubs and weeds and young trees. What happiness to dwell in the grounds of the "shiftless" farmer! Since tidiness, with most cultivators, means the destruction of all natural beauty, and especially the cutting down of everything that interferes with the prosperity of cabbages and potatoes, blessed is untidiness to the lover of Nature. So long as I study birds I shall carefully seek out the farmer who has lost his energy, and allows Nature her own inimitable way in his fields and lanes. The fascinations of that neglected corner cannot be put into words. The whole railroad embankment which bordered it on one side, stretching far above my head, was a mad and joyous tangle of wild-grape vines. In the shade of a cluster of slender trees was a spot enriched by springs, where flourished the greenest of ferns, sprinkled with Jack-in-the-pulpits and forget-me-nots. This was the delight of my heart, and my consolation for the trials connected with chat affairs.

Alas that the usual fate of Nature's divine work should overtake it; that into a "shiftless" head should come the thought that railroad ties and fallen trees make good firewood, and without too much trouble can be dragged out by horses! As a preliminary calamity, half-starved cows were turned in to nibble the grass, and incidentally to trample and crush flowers and ferns into one ghastly ruin. And at the same moment, as if inspired by the same spirit of destruction, some idle railroad "hand," with a scythe, laid low the whole bank of grapevines. Ruthless was the ruin, and wrecked beyond repair the spot, after man's desolating hand passed over it; a scene of violence, of dead and dying scattered over the trampled and torn-up sod; "murder most foul" in the eyes of a Nature-lover. I could not bear to look upon it. I shunned it, lest I should hate my fellow-man, who can, unnecessarily and in pure wantonness, destroy in one hour what he cannot replace in a lifetime.

A TRAGEDY IN THE LANE.

Nor was that the full measure of sufferings inflicted on the lane—and me. That beautiful green passageway happened to be a short cut from the meadow, and horse-rake and hay-wagon made the ravage complete. The one crushed and dragged out every sweet-growing thing spared by the previous devastators, and the other defiled with wisps of dead grass every branch that reached over its grateful shade. It was pitiful, as much for the exhibition thus made of a man's insensible and sordid existence, as for the laceration of my feelings and the actual ruin wrought.

A pleasanter theme is the love-making in which I chanced to catch the beautiful but bewildering pair in the blackberry bushes. Madam, hopping about an old apple-tree, was apparently not in the least interested in her lover, who followed after, in comical fashion, with ludicrous and truly chat-like antics, every feather raised, crouching, with head turned this way and that, and neck stretched out, and changing his position at every hop with the most dramatic action. If modern theories are true, and bird eccentricities of dress and behavior are assumed to please and win the mate, what must we think of the taste of our demure little sisters in feathers?

Did I ever assert that the chat is shy? Then am I properly punished for not appreciating his individuality, by having to admit that this pair possessed not a trace of the quality. The singer seemed to be always on exhibition; and as for his spouse, though she performed no evolutions, she came boldly into sight, postured in the most approved Delsartian style, uttered a harsh purr or jerked out a "mew," with a sidewise fling of her head which showed the inside of her mouth to be black,—all for my benefit, and without the slightest embarrassment. She made it obvious to the dullest understanding, that while she did not like spies, nor approve of human curiosity in neighborhood matters, she was not in the least afraid.

As the days passed on, a change crept over the chat family; they became more retiring. In my daily walk they were not so easily found; indeed, sometimes they were not to be seen at all. When I did discover them, they seemed very much engaged in private affairs, with no time for displays of any sort. No more droll performances on the tree-top, no more misleading antics in the blackberries; the days of frolic were over, the sober duties of life claimed all their energies, and they went about silently and stealthily. Of course I was sure something had happened to induce this change,—no doubt nestlings,— and a great and absorbing determination grew in my mind to find that nest, if I suffered in body and estate from every bush in the patch.

PERSEVERANCE REWARDED.

Let the story of my encounter be veiled in oblivion. Suffice it to say that perseverance under such difficulties deserved, and met, reward. In due time I saw the bird flit away, and my eyes fell upon the nest. No birds, but four pearls of promise within.

"Think on the speed, and the strength, and the glory,
    The wings to be, and the joyous life,
Shut in those exquisite secrets, she brooded."

I looked, but did not touch; and I departed content. A few days later I made another call. Again I flushed the mother from the nest, and this time looked upon a brown mass of wriggling baby chats. Meanwhile, since life had become so serious, the chat sobered down into the dignified head of a family, and joined his mate in hard work from morning till night.

But summer days were passing. Dandelion ghosts lined the paths, wild roses dropped their rosy pink and appeared in sombre green, and meadow lilies peeped out from every fence corner. A few days after my grand discovery, I went one evening to the blackberry tangle, and was greeted by gleeful shouts and calls from the bird of late so silent. There he was, his old self, his recent reserve all gone. My heart fell; I suspected, and in a moment I knew the reason. The nest was empty. Where, then, could be those youngsters, less than a week old, who four days before were blind and bare of feathers? They could not have flown; they must have been hurried out of the nest as soon as they could stand. Could it be because I knew their secret? I felt myself a monster, and I tried to make amends by hunting them up and replacing them. But the canny parents, as usual, outwitted me. Not only had they removed their infants, but they had hidden them so securely that I could not find them, and I was sure, from their movements, that they were not bereaved.

THE TOO CLEVER CHAT.

I began my search by trying to follow the wily singer, who appeared to understand, and regard it as a joke. First he led me up the lane, then I had to follow down the lane; the next minute he shouted from the blackberry patch, and I had to go around the wall to reach him. Alas, the race between wings and feet is hopeless! I abandoned that plan, and resolved to go to a grove not heretofore invaded, being absolutely impenetrable from undergrowth. My way led across a cornfield, over stone walls, through thickets and bushes everywhere. Many other birds I startled, and at last came a chat's "mew" from a wild jungle of ailantus and brambles, which nothing less effective than an axe could pass through. But on I went around the edge, the chat's call accompanying me, and at the point where it sounded loudest I dropped to a humble position, hoping that eyes might enter further than feet. Nothing to be seen or heard but a flit of wings. The singer tried to lead me away, but I was serious and not to be coaxed, and all his manœuvres failed. I seated myself on the ground, for now I heard low, soft baby calls, and determined to stay there till the crack of doom, or till I had solved the mystery of those calls.

But I did not stay so long, and I did not see the babies. An hour or two of watching weakened my determination, and slowly and sadly I wended my way homeward; admiring, while I execrated, the too, too clever tactics of the chat. But I did make one discovery,—that a sound which had puzzled me, like the distant blow of an axe against a tree, must be added to the *répertoire* of the chat mother. I saw her utter it, and saw the strange movement of the throat in doing so. The sound seemed to come up in bubbles, which distended her throat on the outside exactly as if they had been beads as big as shoe buttons.

I was not to be wholly disappointed. Fate had one crumb of consolation for me, for I saw at last a chat baby. He was a quiet, well-behaved little fellow, with streaks on throat and breast, and dull yellow underparts. His manners were subdued, and gave no hint of the bumptious acrobat he might live to be.

While the vagaries of chat life had been drawing me down toward the lane, the feathered world on the other side of the house had not been idle; and glad now to avoid the ruined lane and the deserted berry patch, I turned my attention to a bird drama nearer home, the story of which must have a chapter to itself.

VI.

THE "BIRD OF THE MUSICAL WING."

Mr. Bradford Torrey has started an inquiry into the conduct of the ruby-throated hummingbird, who is said, contrary to the habits of the feathered world in general, to absent himself from his family during the time that his mate is brooding and rearing the young. The question of interest to settle is his motive in so doing. Does he consider his brilliant ruby dangerous to the safety of the nest, and so deny himself the pleasure as well as the pain of family life? Does he selfishly desert outright, and return to bachelor ways, when his mate settles herself to her domestic duties? Or does the pugnacious little creature herself decline not only his advice and counsel, but even his presence?

This problem in the life of the bird has lent new interest to its study, and I was greatly pleased, last summer, when the bursting into bloom of a trumpet creeper, which clad with beauty the branches of an old locust-tree, attracted to the door of my temporary home this

"Rare little bird of the bower,
Bird of the musical wing."

No sooner did the great red trumpets begin to open than their winged admirers appeared, and the special object of my interest—whether by right of discovery or by force of will I could not determine—asserted her claim to the vine and its vicinity, and at once proceeded to evict every pretender to any share of the treasure. Nor was it a difficult task; for though the smallest of our birds, the ruby-throat is perhaps the most spirited. No bird, not even the mighty eagle, standard-bearer of the republic, is too big for this midget to attack, and none fails to retire before his rapier-like beak. Madam of the vine lacked none of the courage and self-assertion of her race, and a few lively skirmishes convinced the neighbors, with one exception, that this particular crop of blossoms was preëmpted and no trespassing allowed. That matter happily arranged, she settled down in peace to enjoy her estate, and I followed her example.

July was nearly half gone when blossoms began to unclose on the vine and my lady took possession. The world about the house and orchard was full of melody, for goldfinches were just celebrating their nuptials, and birds have to furnish their own wedding music. Though a march may express the pomp and ceremony of human marriage, a rhapsody is more in harmony with joyous bird unions, and the air rang with their raptures. The marriage hymn of the hummingbird—if any there were—was not for human ears; indeed, most of the life, certainly all of the wedded life of this bird, is shrouded in mystery, perhaps never to be unraveled till we understand bird language, and can subject him to an "interview."

A TALKATIVE HUMMINGBIRD.

The first thing that surprised me in my little neighbor was her volubility, for I had never found her kin talkative. She made remarks to herself, doubtless both witty and wise, but sounding to her dull-eared hearers, it must be confessed, like squeaky twitters; and somewhat later, when she recognized me as an admirer, as I fully believe she did, she even addressed some conversation to me, going out of her way to fly over my head as she did so.

Nothing could be more dainty than her way of exploring the flowers on her vine. Poising herself on wing before a blossom, she first gazed earnestly into its rosy depths, to judge of its quality,—or possibly of its tenants; for it was not nectar alone that she sought. If it pleased her, she dashed upon it, seized the lower rim with her tiny claws, and folded her wings. Then drawing her head far back, she thrust her beak, her head, and sometimes her whole body into the flower tube, her plump little form completely filling it; and there she hung motionless for a few seconds, while I struggled with the temptation to inclose blossom and bird in my hand. If the flower chanced to be an old one, her roughness sometimes detached it, when she hastily backed out, protesting indignantly, and looking over to see it fall.

Atom though the hummer was, hardly more than a pinch of feathers, she was a decided character, with notions and ways of her own. One of her fancies was to open the honey-pots for herself. When she found a bud beginning to unclose, a lobe or two unfolded, she at once took it in hand and vigorously proceeded to aid the process with her needle-like beak, and the instant it was accomplished rushed in to secure her spoils in their first freshness. She never appeared to have patience to wait for anything, and sometimes even tried to hurry up dilatory buds. She did succeed, as such vehemence must, in breaking in the back way, as it were, through a hole in the corolla tube, and rifling the bud before it had a chance to become a blossom. I could not decide positively whether she pierced the tubes, or availed herself of the labors of an oriole I had seen splitting them by inserting his beak and then opening it wide to enlarge the hole.

A YOUTHFUL INTRUDER.

One quality that my little friend most woefully lacked was repose. Not only were her motions jerky and exasperating in the extreme, but during my whole acquaintance with her I never saw her for a moment absolutely still. On the rare occasions when her body was at rest, her head turned from side to side as though moved by machinery, like the mandarin dolls of the toy-shops, and I had doubts whether she ever slept. I was really concerned about her. Nervous prostration seemed the only thing she could look forward to; and later I found that Bradford Torrey had suffered similar anxiety about one of her kind, as related in his charming story, "A Widow and Twins."

There was one exception, as I said, to the complete success of the little lady in green, in establishing her claim to the vine. The individual who refused to be convinced interested me greatly. He looked a guileless and innocent youth; his tender age being indicated by a purer white on the breast and a not fully grown tail. Moreover, he was not so deft in movement as the experienced matron he defied; he was almost clumsy, in fact, having some difficulty in manœuvring his unwieldy beak and getting his head into the tube, and being much disconcerted by the swaying of the blossoms in the breeze. Youth and innocence were shown, too, in the manner of the little stranger toward my lady. He approached her in a confiding way, as if expecting a welcome, and was plainly astonished at being attacked instead. Indeed, he apparently could not believe his repulse was serious, for he soon returned in the most friendly spirit, and utterly refused to be driven away.

After making myself well acquainted with the manners and ways of Madam Ruby-throat, and noting that she always took her departure in exactly the same direction and at quite regular intervals, I began to suspect that she had important business somewhere; probably a nest, possibly a pair of twin babies. Should I undertake the hopeless task of seeking that tiny lichen-covered cradle, so nearly resembling a thousand knots and other protuberances that one might as easily find the proverbial needle in a hay-stack, or should I turn my attention to other inviting quarters on the place? While I hesitated, balancing the attractions, madam herself chanced to give me a hint. One morning, as I was watching her steady flight across the lawn, I caught a decided upward swerve of the gleaming line, and instantly resolved to take the hint, if such it were. I went quietly to a pear-tree on her course, and waited for the next point, if she chose to give it. She did; she was most obliging,—may I venture to say friendly? Almost immediately she passed me, and alighted on one of a row of tall trees that lined the road. There she hovered for a moment, giving sharp digs at one spot, as though detaching something, and then flew straight along the line to an immense silver poplar.

SHE SHOWED ME THE NEST.

Here at last the bird settled, and a wild hope sprang up in my heart. Stealing nearer to the tree without taking my eyes from the spot; ignoring the danger of pitfalls in my path, of holes to fall into and rocks to fall over, of briers to scratch and snakes to bite, I drew as near as I dared, and then cautiously raised my glass to my eyes, and behold! the nest with my lady upon it! The thrill of that moment none but a fellow bird-lover can understand. What now was the most beguiling of chats; what the danger of dislocating my neck; what the dread of neighborhood wonder; what the annoyance of mosquitoes, or dogs, or small boys, or loose cattle, or anything? There was the nest. (I am obliged to admit, parenthetically, that nearly all these calamities befell me during my devotion to that nest, but I never faltered in my attentions, and I never regretted.)

At the moment of discovery, however, I was too excited to watch. First carefully locating the tiny object by means of a dead branch,—for I knew I should have to seek it again if I lost it then, and the luck of finding it so easily could not fall to me twice,—I rushed to the house to share my enthusiasm with a sympathizer.

My lady ruby-throat was a canny bird; she had selected her position with judgment. The silver poplar of her choice was covered with knobs so exactly copied by the nest that no one would have suspected it of being anything different. It was on a dead branch, so that foliage could not trouble her, while leafy twigs grew near enough for protection. No large limb afforded rest for a human foe, and it was at the neck-breaking height of twenty feet from the ground. Neck-breaking indeed I found it, after a trial of twenty minutes' duration, which, judging from my sensations, might have been a century.

But whether my head ever recovered its natural pose or not, I was happy; for I saw the hummingbird shaping her snug domicile to her tidy form, turning around and around in it, pressing with breast and bend of the wing, as I was certain, from the similarity of her attitude and motions to those of a robin I had closely watched at the same work. During the time I watched her she made ten trips between the poplar and the vine, and at every visit worked at shaping the nest and adjusting the outside material. She did not care for my distant and inoffensive presence on the earth below, and she probably did not suspect the power of my glass to spy upon her secrets, for she showed no discomfiture at my frequent visits. Indeed, she took pains to let me know that she had her eye upon me, for twice when she left the nest she swerved from her course to swoop down over my head, squeaking most volubly as she passed.

A CHARMING SPOT.

While sitting at my post of observation, my neck sometimes refused to retain its unnatural position a moment longer, and then I refreshed myself with other objects around; for after some search I had found a charming place for study. It was beside a rocky ledge which ran through the middle of a bit of meadow-land, and happily defied being cultivated, although it supported a flourishing crop of wildings,—scattering elm, oak, and pine trees, with sumac, goldenrod, and other sweet things to fill up the tangle. Under a low-spreading tree I placed my seat: at my back the screening rocks, in front a strip of meadow waiting for the mower. Along the side where I entered ran a stone wall, but before me was a stretch of delightfully dilapidated old board and pole fence. It had been reinforced and made available for keeping out undesirables by barbed wire, but at my distance that was inconspicuous and did not disturb me. The fence had never been painted, the wind and weather of many years had toned it down to the hue of a tree-trunk, and it was so thoroughly decorated with lichens that it had come to look almost like a bit of nature's work,—if nature could have made anything so ugly. I believe the birds regarded it as a special arrangement for their benefit. Certainly they used it freely.

But beyond the fence was a genuine bit of nature's handiwork in which man had no part: an extended and luxuriant tangle, bordering the river, of alder and other bushes, with here and there a young tree, elm, apple, cedar, or wild cherry; and winding through it a bewitching path, made by cows in their unconventional and meandering style and for their own convenience, penetrating every charming nook in the shrubbery, and so unnoticeable at its entrance that one might pass it and not suspect its presence. In this path bushes met over their heads, often not high enough for ours, wild roses perfumed the air, and meadow-sweet lingered long after it was gone from haunts less cool and shaded. Every turn offered a new and fascinating picture, and a stroll through the irresistible way always began or ended my day's study.

FLOATED OFF THE NEST.

For several days following my happy discovery I spent much time watching domestic affairs in the poplar-tree. The little matron was not a steady sitter. From two to four minutes, at intervals of about the same length, was as long as she could possibly remain in one place; and even then she entertained herself by rearranging the materials composing her nest, till I began to fear she would have it pulled to pieces before the birdlings appeared. Beautiful beyond words was her manner of entering and leaving her snug home. On departing, she simply spread her wings and floated off, as if lifted by the rising tide of an invisible element; and on returning, she sank from a height of ten or twelve inches, as if by the subsidence of the same tide.

This corner of my small world, however enchanting with its rocky ledge, its cow-path, and its nest, did not absorb me entirely. Life about the trumpet-vine was far more stirring and eventful. It was there that madam spent half her time, for at that point, as well as at the nest, were duties to be performed, her larder to be defended, intruders to be banished, and crops to be gathered; there, too, in the intervals, her toilet to be made. That a creature so tiny should make a toilet at all was wonderful to think of, and to see her do it was charming. Each minute feather on gossamer wing or widespread tail was passed carefully through her beak; from all soft plumage, the satin white of the breast and the burnished green of the back, every particle of dust was removed and every disarrangement was set right. Her long white tongue, looking like a bristle, was often thrust out far beyond the beak, and the beak itself received an extra amount of care, being scraped and polished its whole length by a tiny claw, which was used also for combing the head feathers.

At the vine, too, was war; for the youngster already mentioned persisted in denying the matron's right to the whole, and many a sharp tussle they had, when for an hour at a time there would not be a shadow of peace for anybody. Occasionally madam would relax her opposition to the intruder and let him remain on the vine; but with the proverbial ingratitude of beneficiaries, he then assumed to own it himself, and flew at her when she returned from a visit to her nest, as if she had no right there. His advantage lay in having nothing else to do, and thus being able to spend all his time on the ground.

The energy of the little mother was wonderful. In spite of the unrest of her life, of continual struggles, and work over the nest, she frequently indulged in marvelous aerial evolutions, dashing into the air and marking it off into zigzag lines and angles, as if either she did not know her own mind for two seconds at a time, or was forced to take this way to work off surplus vitality.

During all this time I was hoping to see her mate. But if he appeared at all, as several times a ruby-throated individual did, she promptly sent him about his business.

THE WORLD TRANSFORMED.

It was the 19th of July when I decided that sitting had finally begun on the poplar-tree nest, madam controlling her restlessness sometimes for the great space of ten minutes, and working no more on the structure. Now I redoubled my vigilance, going out from the breakfast-table, and spending my day under the rocky ledge, leaving matters at the trumpet-vine to take care of themselves. On the 28th I started out as usual. There had been a heavy fog all night and not a breath of wind stirring, and I found the whole world loaded with waterdrops. When I reached the stone wall which bounded my delightsome field, and slipped through my private gate, I stopped in amazement at the sight before me. The fine meadow-grass was bowed down with its weight of treasure, as if a strong wind had laid it low, and every stem strung its whole length with minute crystals. Purple-flowering grasses turned the infinitesimal gems that adorned every angle into richest amethysts, and looked like jeweled sprays fit for the queen of fairies. Every spider's web was glorified into a net of pearls of many sizes, all threatening, if touched, to mass themselves and run down the tunnel, at the bottom of which, it is to be presumed, sat Madam Arachne waiting for far other prey.

I looked on all this magnificence with admiration and dismay. Should I wade through that sea of gems, which at the touch of my garments would resolve themselves, like the diamonds of the fairy tales, not into harmless dead leaves, but into mere vulgar wet? The hummer flew by to her nest, goldfinches called from the ledge. I hesitated—and went on. Making a path before me with my stick, stepping with care, to disturb no drop unnecessarily, and leaving to every spider her net full of pearls, I reached my usual place, and seated myself in a sea of jewels such as no empress ever wore. And behold, the old fence too was transfigured with strange hieroglyphics, into which dampness had changed the lichens, and one half-dead old tree, under the same subtle influence, had clad its bare and battered branches in royal velvet, of varied tints of green, white, and black.

At last I turned lingeringly from all this beauty to the nest. Ah! something had happened there too! Madam sat on the edge, leaned over, and made some movements within. At my distance I could not be positive, but I could guess —and I did, and subsequent events confirmed me—that birdlings were out. Like other bird mammas, she sat on those infants as steadily as she had sat on the eggs, and it was a day or two later before I saw her feed. This was the murderous-looking fashion in which that dainty sprite administered nourishment to her babies: she clung to the edge of the nest, and appeared to address herself to the task of charging an old-fashioned muzzle-loading gun, using her beak for a ramrod, and sending it well home, violently enough, one would suppose, to disintegrate the nestling on whom she operated. If I had not read Mr. Torrey's description of hummingbird feeding, I should have thought the green-clad dame was destroying her offspring, instead of tenderly ministering to their wants.

A MURDEROUS-LOOKING OPERATION.

Bird babies grow apace. Appetites waxed stronger, and the trumpet-vine had dropped its blossoms. The little mother had to seek new fields, and she settled on a patch of jewel-weed for her supplies. Now, if ever, was needed the help of her mate, but not once did he show himself. Was he loitering—as the books hint—at a distance, and did she go to him now and then, on her many journeys, to tell him how the young folk progressed? I cannot tell; I was busy watching the business partner; I had no time to hunt up absentees. But I have a "theory," which may or may not explain his apparent indifference. It is that the small dame, so intolerant of neighbors even on her feeding-ground, simply cannot endure any one about her, and prefers to do all her building and bringing-up herself, with no one to "bother." Have we not seen her prototype in the human world?

The young hummers had been out of their shells for two weeks before I saw them, and then the sight was unsatisfactory,—only the flutter of a tiny wing, and two sharp beaks thrust up above the edge. But after this day beaks were nearly always to be seen, and sometimes a small round head, or a glistening white tongue, or the point of a wing appeared to encourage me. Baby days were now fast passing away; the mother fed industriously, and the "pair of twins," waxed strong and pert, sat up higher in the nest, and began the unceasing wag of the head from side to side, like their mother. What a fairy-like world was this they were now getting acquainted with! What to them was the presence of human beings, with their interests, their anxieties, and their cares, passing far below on the road, or what even the solitary bird-student, sitting hour after hour by the rocks in silence, turning inquisitive eyes upon them? The green tree was their world, and their mother was queen. Valiantly did this indefatigable personage drive away every intruder, bravely facing the chickadee who happened to alight in passing, even showing fight to the wasps that buzzed about her castle in the air. I shall always think she really knew me, and had a not unfriendly feeling toward me, for when I met her about the place, even away from the nest, she frequently greeted me with what one would not wish to be so disrespectful as to call a squeaking twitter.

THE BABY FLIES.

As the end of the three weeks reported to be necessary to fit baby hummers for life drew near, I rarely left the rocky ledge for an hour of daylight, so anxious was I to see a nestling try his wings. The mother herself seemed to be in a state of expectancy, and would often, after feeding, linger about the little home, as if inviting or expecting a youngster to come out to her. At the last I could not stay in my bed in the morning, but rushed out before sunrise, remembering how momentous are the early morning hours in the bird-world. But it was noon of the twenty-first day of his life when the first baby flew. He had just been fed, and he sat on the edge of the nest beating his wings, when all at once away he went, floating off like a bit of thistledown, up and out of sight. Though expecting it and looking for it, I was greatly startled when the moment came.

The last act in the little drama was a pretty scene in the bushes. I was wandering about in the hope of one more interview, when suddenly my lady and a young one alighted on a twig before me. She appeared to feed the youth, hovered about him an instant, and with the tip of her beak touched him gently on the forehead. Then, with a farewell twitter, both flew away over my head, so closely they almost swept me with their wings. And so the pretty story of the nest was ended.

VII.

MY LADY IN GREEN.

Truly a fairy-like dwelling was that nest on the apple-tree; about the size of a walnut, with one leaf for a shelter. It was placed—I had almost said grew—in a slender crotch of a low-hanging bough. No coarse grass stems or bark fibres bound it to its slight moorings; it seemed to stand by its own fitness, to be a part of the branch itself. Soft, creamy-hued vegetable cotton, pressed and felted into a certain firmness of consistency, formed the structure, and a close covering of lichens held it in shape and completed its beauty, while giving an apple-branch tone that made it almost invisible. An inch in depth and the same in breadth furnished ample quarters for the twin hummingbird babies whose home it was.

But the charm that had drawn me across four States to study it was its situation. For when has one of those airy sprites, with the whole expanse of the tallest trees at command, chosen to come down to the level of mortals, to set up her domestic gods within reach of a human hand, and within hearing of a human ear? What friendly spirit bade her select a scantily leaved branch, backed by the heavy foliage of luxuriant maples, that rendered her fairy-like home conspicuous whatever the weather and wherever the sunlight fell? By what happy thought did she settle upon a low bough with long swaying ends, by which to draw it gently down, and thus let the enraptured bird-lover watch closely day by day the growth and development of her darlings? and so near a house that one could look into it from a window? Long railway trips in dusty August, the hot days and hotter nights of that fiery month, and the various minor discomforts of close summer—boarder quarters were all forgotten in a great joy.

Nothing was ever more bewitching to watch than that atom in feathers, the hummingbird mother. She was so tiny that her life might be crushed out between a thumb and finger, yet she was full of love and anxiety about her birdlings. She was thoughtful in her care of them, and industrious in supplying their wants. In a word, she was a pattern of perfect and beautiful motherhood. Charming it was, beyond expression, to see her come home to her beloved, embroidering angles in the air,—hummingbird fashion,— pausing a dozen times on wing, looking at them from as many points of view, and at length dropping lightly as a feather upon the edge, like a fairy godmother with her gifts of food; and then in a few moments suddenly rise, up—up—up, with body erect as if mounting an invisible ladder, till, at five or six feet above, she shot away so swiftly no eye could follow her.

When startled, as she frequently was in her close proximity to our noisy race, she darted off like a flash, forward or backward, upward or downward, never turning, but dashing in any direction opposite to the quarter from which the disturbance came. On the rare occasions when she was not frightened, she seemed unable to tear herself away. She would hover about her nest, five or six inches from it, this side and that, over and around again, with eyes apparently fixed on her treasures, sometimes daintily touching with the tip of her beak the nest, or one of the nestlings, in a caressing manner.

The small dame too, though wary and easily startled, had a great deal of repose of manner. When settled over her infants, she sat still most of the time, not moving her head from side to side in the restless way of some of her family, but looking straight before her and as quiet as a thrush.

In another way the little mother ignored the traditions; she did not always hum. Until the little ones were ten or twelve days old she came to the nest in perfect silence; after that she began to hum, and by the time they were two weeks old she came with her characteristic note every time.

It is interesting to see how all birds recognize and respect the right of a mother to her own tree, or the part of a tree on which she has set up her home. Big birds like robins and thrashers, even belligerent ones, who will not generally allow themselves to be driven, usually depart speedily before the beak of the least of mothers asserting her ownership of a tree or bush; not because they are afraid of her, but because they appreciate the justice of her title, and demand the same for themselves.

Small as was the apple-tree dweller, she had managed, before I knew her, to establish her claim to her own vicinity. Goldfinches and yellow warblers, vireos and robins, were about; I heard them on all sides, but not one intruded upon her tree or the neighboring sides of the maples. As the young progressed and waxed bumptious, she became more and more cautious. She made many more angles and observations in the air before alighting, looking at them from every possible side, as if wishing to assure herself that nothing had happened in her absence. She even resented the presence under her tree of a hen and chickens, and flew at them with savage cries. But the barnyard matron was too much absorbed in her own maternal anxieties to pay any heed to the midget buzzing and squeaking around her head; and madam herself seemed to appreciate the absurdity of her proceeding, for in a moment she returned to her duties, and remonstrated no more.

How shall I picture the growth and development of the twins in that cherished home! Where shall I find words delicate and subtle enough to describe the change as I saw it from day to day, from puny atoms the size of a honey-bee to fledged and full-grown hummingbirds! Every morning, watching and waiting till the whole of our little world was at breakfast, I drew down the fateful branch and indulged in a long, close look at them, and no language at my command is adequate to describe the process of unfolding.

At first sight of the two I was lost in amazement. Could those minute, caterpillar-like objects, covered with scanty and scattering hairs, lying side by side in the bottom of their miniature cradle, be the offspring of the winged sprites of the bird-world? Would those short, wide, duck-like beaks ever become the needle-shaped probers of flowers? Would wings ever grow on those grub-like bodies? They were at this time four and five days old; for though they appeared like twins, I learned from previous watchers that there was a day's difference between them.

After I had looked and wondered, and returned to my seat behind the window-blinds to watch, the mother came to feed. It would be pleasant to imagine that the food brought by that dainty dame, and administered to her beloved brood, consisted of the nectar of flowers, drawn from the sweet peas that filled the garden with beauty and perfume, the gay flaunting scarlet beans over the way, or the golden drops of the jewel-weed modestly hiding under their broad leaves, in the hollow down by the bridge. But Science, in her relentless substitution of fact for fancy, does not allow us this agreeable delusion. Something far more substantial, not to say gross, we are informed, is required to build up the muscle and bone of the atoms in the nest. Meat is what they must have, and meat it was, in the shape of tiny spiders and perhaps other minute creatures, that mamma was seeking when she hovered under the maple boughs, now and then touching a twig or the underside of a leaf. Indeed, one might occasionally see her pick off her spider as deftly as one would pick a peach.

Hummingbird feeding has been graphically described more than once; but when the food-bearer arrived I seized my glass, eager to see it again. This is the way my fairy-like mother administered the staff of life to her tender birdlings. Alighting on the edge of the nest, she leaned over, and with her beak jerked a little head into sight above the edge; then down the baby's throat she thrust her long beak its whole length; and it looked actually longer than the youngster itself. Then she prodded and shook the unfortunate nestling, who seemed to hold on, till I wondered his head did not come off. It was truly fearful to witness. In a moment, shaking off, apparently with difficulty, that one, who dropped out of sight, she jerked up the other, and treated it in the same rough way, shaking her own body from head to tail by her exertion. Thus alternately she fed them, three or four times, before she finished; and then she calmly slipped on to the nest, wriggling and twisting about as if she were pawing them over with her feet. There she sat for five or six minutes before darting away for fresh supplies, while I wondered if the two victims of this Spartan method were lying dead, stabbed to death, or smothered, by their own mother. But I did her tenderness and her motherhood injustice. Regularly every half hour she came and repeated this murderous-looking process, unless, as often happened, she was frightened away by the people about.

Till her little ones were two weeks old, the devoted if apparently ungentle parent continued to feed them at intervals of thirty minutes, the neck-dislocating performance being always as violent as I have described. After that date she came more frequently, every fifteen or twenty minutes, and their development went on more rapidly. At the early age of five and six days, even before their eyes were open, the young birds began to show that they had minds of their own, and knew when they had enough (which some folk bigger than birds never know). When one was sufficiently filled, or sufficiently racked, it would shut its mouth and refuse to open, though mamma touched it gently with her beak.

"The world slipped away and I was in fairyland," wrote my old friend the Enthusiast, while watching, in another part of the country that same summer, the nest-building of a hummingbird. To me, also, the study of the life and affairs of this nest, to which I gave nearly every hour of daylight for weeks, seemed like a glimpse into that land of childhood's dreams, excepting when the outer world obtruded too rudely. For the life that went on under and around that charmed spot was far from fairy-like. The "hard facts" of human existence were ever uppermost, and there were a thousand disturbances between breakfast and bedtime. Indeed, the nest was the neighborhood show; everybody longed to pull down the branch and look at it. Men, women, and boys; master, mistress, and maids; horses, cattle, and birds, conspired to keep up an excitement around the apple-tree. It seemed a magnet to draw to itself all the noise and confusion of that peaceful village.

THE NEIGHBORHOOD SHOW.

There was the man who assumed the office of showman, brought a chair out under the tree, pulled down the branch, and invited every passer-by to step up and look, with the comment, "Big business raising such a family as that!" while I sat in terror, dreading lest the branch slip from his careless fingers and fling the little ones out into the universe, an accident I saw befall a chipping sparrow's brood, as already related.

There, too, was the horse who halted under the tree and regaled himself with apples which he gathered for himself, jerking his branch violently; happily not *the* branch, or there would have been a sudden end to dreams of fairyland.

Above all, there were the summer boarders, to whom in that quiet rural life any object of interest was a godsend and greedily welcomed. Every day, and many times a day, a procession passed on the way to the "Springs" of odorous —not to say odious—memory, equipped with tumblers and cups, pitchers and pails, and every one paused at the little show in front of the house, where, alas! there was no fence. Well dressed city women stopped, and stared, and pointed with parasols, often asking for a look into the nest.

All this hindered the poor little mother in her domestic duties. She would come near, alight on a twig far above, and wait, hoping to reach her darlings, till some laugh or movement startled her away; and usually just before dark, while the village was at supper, she had to feed very often to make up for short commons all day.

There were other dangers too, which I hoped did not worry the "wee birdie" as they did me. Two or three times a strong wind—a November gale out of date, rocked and tossed that tiny cradle all day, while I frequently held my breath, in fear of seeing the twins flung out. But the canny little creatures cuddled down in the nest, which by that time seemed too small to hold them, showing only beaks and, later, immature tails above the edge.

Once, very early in their lives, came a steady rain. All night long the devoted mother received the downpour on her back, and all the next day, with short intervals of food-seeking, she remained at her post, while the water ran off her tail in streams. She kept her younglings warm and dry, but the nest was sadly damaged, the lichen covering was softened and brightened in color, and the whole structure spread and settled, so that I feared it would not hold together till the little ones were grown.

A MALICIOUS-LOOKING APPLE.

There, too, was the ever-present menace of falling apples, which were constantly dropping from the tree. A well-loaded branch hung over the nest, and one particularly malicious-looking specimen of an angry reddish hue, suspended as it appeared exactly above, had a deep dimple in one side which gave it a sinister expression, and one could not help the suspicion that it might delight in letting go its hold and dashing that frivolous nursery to the ground.

The very leaves themselves appeared to show character. I was never so impressed by their behavior, though I had previously seen some curious performances that looked very much as if leaves have minds of their own. Three inches from the little homestead grew a twig bearing a clump of leaves, perhaps five or six. When I began watching, the largest one hung closely over the nest, on the side toward my window, so that part of the time the whole affair was hidden from sight. In the interest of Science (in whose name, as well as in the name of Liberty, many crimes are committed), I thought it necessary quietly to remove that leaf. Then, although the remainder of the bunch still hung over the nest, two or three inches above, my view was perfect, for I could look under them. Strange to say, however, in a day or two I noticed that another leaf had begun to droop over the tiny homestead. In the morning and again in the afternoon, it held itself well up out of my way, but when the sun was hot in the middle of the day, it fell lower and lower, till it was almost as good a screen as its elder brother had been. Nor was that the end of its vagaries. When a strong wind came up from the south, that leaf drew closer, and actually hugged the nest, so that I could not see it at all. I longed to remove it, but I had not the heart to deprive the nestlings of their shelter. Strangest of all leaf eccentricities, however, was the conduct of another one of the same clump, which during a northwest gale came down at the back, and somehow wedged itself between the nest and branch, so that it formed a perfect shield on that side, so snug indeed that the mother could hardly get under it to feed her little ones. And so it remained all day, during a wind that threatened to blow the whole tree down. I am aware that this will be hard to credit. But I examined it carefully; I know the mother did not arrange it, and I do not exaggerate in the slightest degree.

GROWING UP.

Let me picture the apple-tree babies at one week old, or seven and eight days respectively—to be exact. On taking my regular morning observation I noticed white spine-like processes, the beginning of feathers, among the hairs on their bodies. The heads looked as if covered with, in the language of commerce, a "fine mix," minutest possible white specks on a black ground, which, as days went by, increased in size and length till they developed into feathers. Beaks, too, were changing. The broad, flat surface showed inclination to draw into a point at the tip, which would go on stretching up day by day, till by the time the birdlings could fly they would be nearly as well equipped for hummingbird life as the mother herself. On that seventh day, also, I discovered the first voluntary movement; one of the pair lifted his head above the edge of the nest, and changed his position on the bed of cotton.

Now began the restlessness characteristic of our smallest bird. From the age of one week they were rarely for a moment still, excepting when asleep. One moment they would lie side by side, two tiny beaks sticking up close together, and the next, one would struggle and twist about till his beak showed on the opposite side. Occasionally one made himself comfortable by lying across his fellow, but very soon the lower one squirmed out from under. At nine days they filled the nest so full that their bodies showed above the edge, and gave it the appearance from my window of being filled with hairy and very restless caterpillars.

The eighth and the ninth day of their little lives opened their eyes on the beautiful green world about them, and backs began to look ragged, as if feathers were at hand. Character was developing also. When mamma touched a closed beak in invitation to lunch, it would sometimes respond with a quick little jerk, as who should say, "Let me alone!" or "Don't bother me!" and on this day began also the attempt to dress the feathers yet to appear, and the running out of the bristle-like tongue.

A great surprise awaited me on the fifth day of my enchanting study, the tenth of their life. When I paid my morning visit to the bewitching pair, lying, as always now, close up to the edge of their frail cup, they looked at me with clear, calm black eyes, and saluted me in low, plaintive voices. I should hardly have been more startled if they had spoken to me.

LIKE BUNDLES OF RAGS.

They assumed a new attitude also toward mamma, refusing to allow her to crush them down into the nest and sit upon them, as if they were babies still. They would keep their heads up, and sometimes she really had a struggle in taking her old place on the nest. Apparently it is with humming as with some human mothers, hard to realize that their offspring are no longer infants. On one occasion it looked as if the two united in their rebellion and pushed her away, for she actually lost her balance and plunged forward off the nest. She recovered herself almost instantly, but it was a real tumble for the moment. At eleven days began the flutter of wings that should hardly rest in life. Shadowy little things they were, lifted above the nest and waved rapidly a few seconds at a time.

As the interesting nestlings approached the end of their second week, I began to be concerned about the frail walls of their cradle. They had become so lively in movements that it rocked and swayed in its place, and on one side the cotton protruded through its lichen cover. I dreaded to see a little foot thrust out at this point, and wondered if my clumsy fingers could perform the delicate task of replacing it.

On the morning they were two weeks old a strong wind set in from the northwest, and I drew down the branch with dread of finding it empty. The younglings were wide awake, though settled down into the nest. They looked at me and uttered their soft cries. They now resembled bundles of rags, for feathers were breaking out all over them in the well-defined pattern or design I had observed for several days. Tiny tail feathers with white tips showed distinctly, and it was evident that they were fast growing up. The mother plainly accepted the fact, for she made no further effort to sit upon them.

As the day wore on the wind increased to a gale, and my anxiety kept pace with its violence. Surely no August babies could be prepared for such November weather. Would a fall kill the delicate birdlings? Should I have to rescue them? Hardly five minutes at a time did I take my eyes off the nest, tossed on its long swaying branch like a ship in the maddest sea. Even the mother was blown off the edge, and I rejoiced that she had chosen the south side of the tree, for the north side branches were thrown upward and over with a violence that would have shaken off the nest itself.

But the two sturdy youngsters sat all day with heads up, and tails just showing above the edge, looking out on the raging sea of leaves and riding the storm like veterans. Only once did I see one try to change his position, and then for a second I thought he was lost; but he recovered himself and made no more rash attempts.

SHE ALIGHTED ON THEIR BACKS.

From this day the twins no longer stayed in the nest, but took their position across the top, resting on the edges. By the sixteenth day tails had attained respectable dimensions, and they were clad in the complete dress of feathers, though, having not as yet learned to manage their garments, individual feathers stood out all over and were blown by every breeze into tiny green ripples. In their new position across the top they of course entirely covered the edge, so that the mother was puzzled to find a place for her feet when she came to feed, until she took to alighting on the backs of her monopolizing offspring.

All through these delightful days I had kept a sharp lookout for the father of this charming family, for, as is well known, there is a charge against the ruby-throat, that he takes no part in the home life, that he never visits the nest.

Whether it be that he is too gay a rover to attend to his duties, whether—as is said of the turkey and some other birds—he is possessed of a rage for destroying his own young, whether he keeps out of sight as a measure of prudence for the safety of the nest, or whether that fearless and industrious little mate of his feels capable of managing her own affairs and so drives him away, no one has as yet been rash enough to say. That remains for future observers to find out. The points most interesting to discover at present are, if it is a fact that he never shows himself; if he remains in the neighborhood, and joins his family later, as has been asserted; or if he resumes his care-free bachelor life, and sees them no more.

Only three times was my close watch for visiting hummingbirds rewarded, and those were not at all conclusive. One morning, attracted by the shimmering floor of jewel which Lake Champlain presented under the morning sun, I sat looking out over my neighbor's cornfield, where goldfinch babies were filling the air with their quaint little two-note cries, absorbed in the lovely view, when suddenly I heard a whir of wings and looked up to see a hummer flying about near the nest where madam was sitting. It made two or three jerks, approaching within six inches, and then darted away. Instantly she followed, but not as if in pursuit. There were no cries. It seemed to me a friendly move, an invitation and a response. Alert as she was, she must have seen the stranger, as he—or she—hovered about, yet she did not resent it. In a few minutes she returned and settled herself on her nest.

GREETING ME WITH CRIES.

Soon I heard the familiar sound again, and a bird dashed past the window, not going near the nest. My little dame in the apple-tree paid no attention. An hour later a hummingbird appeared, perhaps the same one, without flying near the apple-tree. Madam left her nest and they had a chase, both passing out of sight. In neither case was there any show of anger, cries, loud hum, or savage rushes, as I have seen when hummingbirds are on the war-path. In neither case, also, could I see the visiting bird plainly enough to determine the sex. It may have been the missing spouse, but then, also, it may not have been.

Nor did it trouble me that I could not solve the mystery. Very early in my study of birds I learned to be content to let many things remain unknown, hoping that some future day would reveal them, and to enjoy what Nature offers me to-day without mourning over things she *this time* withholds.

August was drawing to an end, and claims from the outer world grew clamorous. It wrung my heart to abandon those babies before they could fly, but relentlessly the days went by. The last one arrived, and I went out for a farewell look at the little ones, now eighteen and nineteen days old. They sat as usual side by side across the nest, and greeted me with their sweet little cries. They were completely feathered, though here and there one of the infantile hairs still stuck up between the plumage, the backs a golden green, and the throat and breast snowy white. They returned my gaze with wide, calm eyes, and did not shrink from the finger which gently stroked their backs. The home which had held them was almost a complete wreck, hardly more than a flattened platform, but they clung to it still, and I knew that I should miss the sight I longed for, the first flight. I stayed all day, putting off the parting till the last possible moment, watching and hoping; but when I started for the night train, I left the pair still sitting on the ruins of their nest. And thus ended the only glimpse into fairyland I shall ever enjoy.

A few days later came to me, several hundred miles away, the word that the elder bird (who was a Sunday baby) had taken flight the day he was three weeks old, and had stayed about his native apple-tree all day, while the younger clung to the wreck for two days more, and no one chanced to see him fly.

VIII.

YOUNG AMERICA IN FEATHERS.

"How like are birds and men!" said Emerson, and if he had known nature's loveliest creatures as well as he did his own race, he might have affirmed it more emphatically; for to know birds well is to be astonished at the "human nature" they display.

In our latitude July is distinctly the babies' month. When wild roses give place to sun-kissed meadow lilies, when daisies drop their petals and meadow-sweet whitens the pastures, when blueberries peep out from their glossy coverts and raspberries begin to redden on the hill, then from every side come the baby cries of younglings just out of the nest, and everywhere are anxious parents hurrying about, seeking food to stuff hungry little mouths, or trying to keep too venturesome young folk out of danger. For Young Americans in feathers are wonderfully like Young Americans in lawn in self-confidence and recklessness.

One evening in a certain July, up on the coast of Maine, I watched the frantic efforts of a pair of Maryland yellow-throats—tiny creatures in brown and gold—to coax their self-willed offspring to a more retired position than he chose to occupy. With genuine "Young America" spirit he scorned the conservatism of his elders. Though both parents hovered about him, coaxing, warning, perhaps threatening, not a feather stirred; stolid and wide-eyed he stood, while the father flitted about the bush in great excitement, jerking his body this way and that, flirting his wings, now perking his tail up like that of a wren, again opening and closing it like a fan in the hands of an embarrassed girl, and the mother added her entreaties to his, darting hither and thither, calling most anxiously,—both, in their distress, rashly exposing themselves to what might, for all they knew, be one of the death-dealing machines we so often turn against them.

Nothing had the slightest effect upon the yellow-throated youngster until his own sensations interested him, and his parents suddenly acquired new importance in his horizon. When hunger assailed him, and, looking about for supplies, he spied his provider on the next bush with a beak full of tempting (and wriggling) dainties, and when he found his wily parent deaf to his cries, and understood that not until he flew behind the leafy screen could he receive the food he craved, then he yielded, and joined his relieved relatives out of my sight.

Many times after that morning did the vagaries of that young yellow-throat give me opportunity to study the ways of his family. Having newly escaped from the nursery, in a thorny bush behind thick-growing alders, his strongest desire apparently was to see the world, and those outlying dead twigs, convenient for the grasp of baby feet, were particularly attractive to him. Every day for nearly a week, as I passed into the quiet old pasture, I stopped to interview the youngster, and always found him inquisitive, and evidently, in his own estimation, far wiser than his elders, who were nearly wild over his conduct.

This pasture of about forty acres, lying behind my temporary home, was the joy of my heart, being delightfully neglected and fast relapsing into the enchanting wildness of nature. In a deep bed fringed with a charming confusion of trees and bushes ran a tiny stream, which in the spring justified its right to the title of river. Scattering clumps of alders and young trees of many kinds made it a birds' paradise, while wild cherries and berries of all sorts, with abundant insect life, offered a spread table the whole summer long.

Of flowers it was the chosen home. From the first anemone to the last goldenrod standing above the snow, there was a bewildering confusion; fragrant with roses in June, gorgeous with meadow lilies in July, and rank upon rank of budded goldenrod promising glory enough for August, with all the floral hosts that accompany them. Great patches of sweet bayberry, yielding perfume if only one's garments swept it, and rich "cushions of juniper" frosted over with new tips, were everywhere, and acres were carpeted with lovely, soft, gray-colored moss, into which one's foot sank as into the richest product of the loom. Here and there was a close grove of young pines, whose cool, dim depths were most alluring on hot days; and indeed in every spot in Maine not fully occupied nature is sure to set a pine-tree.

Every morning, on entering this garden of delights, I hastened across an open space by the gate, and plunged into a thicket of alders sprinkled with young trees,—birch, elm, and wild cherry. Through this ran a path, and in a sheltered nook under a low pine I found a seat, where for many days I spent the forenoon, making acquaintance with the pretty little yellow-throats.

From the first the head of the family adopted me as his particular charge, and I am positive he never lost sight of me for one minute. His was a charming surveillance. He did not, like the robin on similar duty, stand on some conspicuous perch like a statue of horror or dismay, uttering his loudest "peep! peep!" in warning to the whole feathered world; nor did he, after the fashion of the song sparrow, fill the air with distressed "pips" that seemed to hint of mischief dire; neither did he, as does the red squirrel, resent an intrusion into preserves that he considered his own, with a maddening series of choking cries, coughs, and "snickers," till one was almost ready to turn a gun upon him; still less did he, in veery style, utter wails so despairing that one felt herself a monster for remaining. The yellow-throat's guardianship was a pleasure. He remained in sight, not fifteen feet away from me, and did not flinch from the terrible field-glass. Sometimes he stood quite still, uttering his soft and inoffensive "chic;" again he scrambled about in the bushes, collected a mouthful, and disappeared for a moment,—a constant baby call from the bushes reminding him of his duty as provider. Evidently he had succeeded in impressing upon that obstinate offspring of his that he must keep out of sight. I wonder what sort of a bugaboo he made me out to be?

Much of the time the tiny custodian passed away in calling and singing, throwing his head up or holding it still according as he sang loud or low. To all varieties of his pretty little melody he treated me. Never once did he utter the notes given in the books as the family song. From his beak I never heard either "wichita," "witches here," "o-wee-chee," or "I beseech you," all of which, excepting the last, I have heard at different times from other members of the family; which, by the way, confirms my oft-repeated assertion that no two birds of a species sing alike. His ordinary notes resembled "pe-o-we," delivered in lively manner, with strong accent on the first syllable. Sometimes he gave them the regulation three times; again, he added a fourth repetition, and changed this by ending on the first syllable of the fifth utterance. On one occasion he surprised and delighted me by turning from the third "pe-o-we" into a continuous little carol, varied and bewitching. Later in the season, after I had finished my studies in the alder bushes, I heard several times from a yellow-throat in the pasture a similar continuous song, usually delivered on the wing.

A QUEER SUN-BATH.

After some days my little watcher became so accustomed to my silent presence under the pine that he did not mind me in the least, though he never forgot me, and if I stirred he was on the alert in an instant. So long as I was motionless he ignored me entirely, and conducted himself as if he were alone; often taking a sunning by crouching on the top twig of a bush, spreading wings and tail and fluffing out his plumage till he looked like a ragged bunch of feathers. It was very droll to see him, while in this attitude, suddenly pull himself together, stand upright, utter his song, and instantly relapse into the spread-eagle position to go on with his sunbath. To my surprise, I found that this warbler, whose song and movements always seem to indicate a constant flitting and scrambling about in warbler fashion, is capable of repose. He frequently stood perfectly still, the black patch which covers his eyes like an old-fashioned face-mask turned toward me, singing his little aria with as much composure as ever thrush sang his.

My pleasing acquaintance with the yellow-throat ended as soon as the young became expert on the wing and could leave their native alder patch. After that the nook was deserted, and unless I heard the song I could not distinguish my little friend among the dozens of his species who lived in the neighborhood.

Toward the north end of my delectable hunting-ground was a second favorite spot, especially attractive on warm, sunny mornings. When I turned my steps that way, I came first upon the feeding-ground of another party of Young Americans,—thrashers. They were a family group, a pair with their two full-grown but still babyish young. Approaching cautiously, I usually found the parents on the ground busily hunting insects, and the youngsters following closely, ready to receive every morsel discovered. They were, however, very well bred, with none of the vulgar manners of those who scream and shout and demand their rations. Later in the day I often found the thrasher singing, a little beyond the alders, on the breezy heights of Raspberry Hill. His chosen place was an almost leafless birch-tree, a favorite perch with all the birds of the pasture, and there he sang for hours.

> "'Twas a song that rippled and reveled and ran
> Ever back to the note whence it began,
> Rising and falling, and never did stay,
> Like a fountain that feeds on itself all day."

Sometimes the singing was interrupted, for those canny Young Americans knew their father's song, and though he had doubtless stolen away and left them foraging on the grass by the path, they heard his voice and came after. While he was pouring out his soul in ecstasy, and I was listening with equal joy, those youngsters came by easy stages nearer and nearer, till one after the other alighted on the lower part of the birch, and, hopping upward from branch to branch, suddenly presented themselves before him, begging in pretty baby fashion for something to eat. The singer, embarrassed by their demands, would sometimes dive into the nearest bushes, followed instantly by the persistent beggars, and in a moment fly off, the infants still in his wake. But he always managed in some way to elude them. Perhaps he fed them or conducted them back to their mother, for in a few minutes he appeared again on the birch and resumed his music.

OUTALONE.

On one occasion I met one of these spruce young thrushes, evidently out on his travels alone for the first time. He was in a state of great excitement,—

76

jerked himself about, "huffed" at me, then flew with some difficulty into a tree, where he stood and watched me in a charmingly naïve and childlike manner, utterly forgetting that part of his education which bade him beware of a human being.

After passing the home of the thrashers, on my usual morning walk toward the north, my next temptation to linger came from a fern-lined path to the spring, abode of other Young Americans. The path itself was extremely seductive, narrow, zigzagging through a small forest of the greenest and freshest of ferns, so luxuriant that they were brushed aside in passing, and closed behind as if to conceal one's footsteps. Shrubs and trees met overhead; here and there a blooming dogbane or an elder, "foamed o'er with blossoms white as snow," and tall wild roses wherever they could find space to grow.

Nearly down to the spring, I seated myself under the bushes and waited. At first, until the bustle of my coming was hushed, all was silent; but soon bird notes began,—soft little "pips" and "chur-r-r's," and other sounds I could not trace to their authors, but plainly expressing disapproval of a spy among them. Catbirds complained with a soft liquid "chuck" or their more decided "mew;" kingbirds peeped out to see what was the excitement, and then settled in the bushes in plain sight, at leisure now since their decorous little folk were educated and taking care of themselves; and other birds came whispering about behind my back, while I dared not turn to see, lest I send everybody off in a panic. An oriole,

"Like an orange tulip flaked with black,"

dropped in as he passed, but left in haste, as if averse to company, with his customary shyness while training the young; for this brilliant bird, during nesting so fearless everywhere, manages to disappear completely after the young leave the nest. Now and then he may be seen going about near the ground, silent, and absorbed in his arduous task of teaching those clamorous urchins to get their own living; or in the early morning, engaged in picking open the hideous nests of the tent-caterpillars and quietly taking his breakfast therefrom. Later, when bantlings are off his mind, he reappears in his favorite haunts, and sings a little before bidding us adieu for the season; although occasionally this supplementary song is a dismal failure, and the oriole discovers, as have other singers before him, that one cannot neglect his music, even for the best of reasons, and take it up again where he left off.

As I passed under an apple-tree, one morning, on my way to the ferny path, I heard the domestic cry of the oriole, uttered, I think, only when rearing the young, a tender "yeap." I paused instantly, and soon heard a very low baby cry, a soft "chur-r-r" exactly like the first note of the young oriole when he comes up to the edge of the nest, only subdued almost to a whisper, showing that education had progressed, and this little one had learned to control his infantile eagerness. All at once there arose a great commotion over my head; an oriole fled precipitately to another tree and stood there watching me, scolding his harshest, flirting his wings and jerking his body in great excitement. In a moment his mate joined him, and both began to call, though she held a worm in her beak. This not seeming to effect their purpose, the singer suddenly uttered a loud, clear whistle of two notes, startlingly like a man's whistle to a dog, when instantly a young oriole flew out of the apple-tree and joined his parents. Then the low note began again, and the family departed.

The infant who receives such devoted care is a pretty little creature in dull yellow, and the most persistent cry-baby I know in the bird-world, though several are not far behind him in this accomplishment. His plaint begins when he mounts the edge of the nest preparatory to his début, and ceases hardly a minute for days, a long-drawn shuddering wail, that suggests nothing less than great suffering, starvation, or some other affliction hard to be borne. What makes the case still worse, the nursery is high, and each nestling chooses for himself the direction in which he will depart. East and west, north and south, they scatter; and where one lands, there he will stay for hours, if not days, drawn down into a little heap, looking lonely and miserable, and apparently impressed with the sole idea that he must keep himself before the world by his voice, or he will be lost and forgotten. It is no wonder that, between the labor of collecting food and following up the family to administer it, the mother becomes faded and draggled, and the father abandons his music, and goes about near the ground, grubbing like any ditch-digger.

The young oriole, however, does not lack intelligence. A correspondent tells me of one who, starting out too ambitiously in his first flight, landed on the ground instead of on the tree he had selected, and, looking about for a place of safety, saw a single leaf growing a few feet up on the trunk of a tree. That so inexperienced an infant should notice it was surprising, but that he should at once start for it showed remarkable "mother wit." To reach this haven of refuge, he ascended the tree-trunk a few inches, half flying and half climbing, clinging with his claws to the bark to rest, then scrambling upward a few inches farther, and so on till he reached the leaf, when he perched on its tiny stem, and remained there as long as he was watched.

But to return to my place among the ferns. When I had been there some time, silent and motionless, a catbird at my back, too happy to be long still, would take courage and charm me with his wonderful whisper song, an ecstatic performance which should disarm the most prejudiced of his detractors. Occasionally, his mate, as I supposed, uttered warning cries, and in deference to her feelings, as it appeared, his notes dropped lower and lower, till I could scarcely hear them, though he was not ten feet away. The song of the catbird is rarely appreciated; probably because he seldom gives a "stage performance," but sings as he goes about his work. In any momentary pause a few liquid notes bubble out; on his way for food, a convenient fence post is a temptation to stop a moment and utter a snatch of song. His manner is of itself a charm, but there is really a wonderful variety in his strains. He has not perhaps so fine an organ as his more celebrated relative, the thrasher; he cannot, or at least he does not, usually produce so clear and ringing a tone.

Nor is his method the same; he does not so often repeat himself, but varies as he sings, so that his aria is full of surprises and unexpected turns. Doubtless, persons expert at finding imitations of other birds' notes would discover some in his. But I am a little skeptical on the subject of conscious "mocking." When the catbird sings I hear only the catbird, and in the same way I take pleasure in the song of thrasher or mockingbird, nor care whether any other may have hit upon his exact combinations.

After the catbird, silence, broken only by the soft, indescribable utterances that are at the same time the delight and the despair of the bird-student. Some birds, upon entering this solitary retreat, announced themselves by a single note, or call, as effectually as if they had sent in a card, while others stole in, took quick and close observation, and departed as quietly as they had come, unseen and unheard by clumsy human senses. Often, indeed, have I wished for eyes to look behind me, where it sometimes seems that everything most interesting takes place.

ANXIOUS DAYS IN CROWLAND.

This secluded corner of the pasture proved to be a very popular nursery with the feathered world. Catbirds came about bearing food, and all sorts of catbird talk went on within hearing: the soft liquid "chuck" and "mew" (so called, though it is more like "ma-a") in all tones and inflections, complaining, admonishing, warning, and caressing. There was evidently a whole family among the bushes. A vireo baby, plainly just out of the cradle, stared at me, and addressed me with a sort of husky squawk, an indescribable sound, which, until I became familiar with it, brought me out in hot haste to see what terrible tragedy was going on. For it is really a distressful cry, although it often proclaims nothing more serious than that the young vireo wants his dinner; as some infants of the human family scream at the top of their voices under similar circumstances.

Beyond the close-growing bushes I heard the crow baby's quavering cry; and these seemed indeed anxious days in crowland. All the little folk were crying at once, in their loudest and most urgent tones, enough to distract the hard-working parents who hurried back and forth overhead, at their best speed, trying to stop the mouths of their ill-bred brood. On one occasion I saw an old crow flying over, calling in a decided, "stern parent" style, followed by a youngster not yet expert on the wing, who answered with his droll baby "ma-a-a" in a much higher key. She was conducting him over the pasture to the salt marsh, where much crow-baby food came from in those days, and he was doing his best to keep up with her stronger flight. Sometimes another sound from the nursery came to my ears,—the caw of an adult, drawn out into a long, earnest "aw-w-w," like admonishing or instructing the now silent olive branches. It was many times repeated, and occasionally interrupted by a baby voice, showing that the little ones were not asleep. I suspect, from what I have seen of crow ways, that the sable mamma is a strict disciplinarian who will tolerate no liberties and no delinquencies on the part of her dusky brood, and although this particular Young American may complain, he dare not rebel. Poor crowling! he needs perhaps a Spartan training to fit him for his hard life in the world. With every man's hand against him, and danger lurking on all sides, he must be wary and sharp and have all his wits about him to live.

THE HEAVENLY SONG.

When I could tear myself away from this domestic corner of the pasture, I passed on to the riverside nook I have mentioned. Here my seat was on the edge of the bank, high above the stream, shaded by a group of black and battered old spruces that looked as if they had faced the storms of a hundred stern Maine winters, as probably they had. Pine-trees at my back filled the air with odors; a thicket beloved of small birds stretched away at one side. Across the river spread a sunny knoll, on which stood a huge old apple-tree, contemporary perhaps with the spruces, having one attractive dead branch, and surrounded at a little distance with a semi-circle of shrubs and low trees. It was a tempting theatre for bird dramas, which the solitary student, half hidden on the bank above, could overlook and bring to clear vision with a glass, while not herself conspicuous enough to startle the actors. In this lovely spot many mornings of that happy July passed delightfully away.

In the leafy background to the apple-tree dwelt the veery. From its apparently impenetrable depths came his warning calls, and on rare and blessed occasions his heavenly song; for it was July, and it is only in June that

"New England woods at close of day,

80

With that clear chant are ringing."

For, with all the rhapsody in his soul, this thrush is a devoted parent, and notwithstanding the fact that he is one of the kings of song, he comes down like the humblest sparrow of the fields, to help feed and train his lovely tawny brood. Without exception that I know, he is the most utterly heartbroken of birds when the nest is discovered. So pathetic are the wails of both parents that I never could bear to study a nest, and I had to harden my heart against the bleating, despairing cries of the mother before I could secure even a look at a youngster just out of the nest. This scion of the charming thrush family is a patient little soul, with all the dignity and reserve as well as the gentleness of his race; no human child could be more winning.

A beautiful instance might be seen in that spot of Nature's provident way of looking out for the future. Those battered old spruces had a flourishing colony of young trees growing up all around and under the shade of their wings, and some day when a great wind breaks off the decayed old ones, there will be several vigorous half-grown young, to take their place, so the place will not be left desolate a day. If man would only take this hint in his own treatment of trees, leave the young ones to take the place of those he removes, we should not have to dread the wasteful destruction of our forests.

A CATBIRD BLUEBERRYING.

In this corner, one morning, I saw a catbird gathering blueberries for dinner. She came down on a fence post as light as a feather, looked over to where I sat motionless under my tree, hesitated, flirted her tail expressively as who should say, "Can I trust her?" then glanced down to the berry-loaded bushes on the ground, and turned again her soft dark eyes on me. I hardly breathed, and she flew lightly to the first wire of the fence, paused, then to the second, still keeping an eye my way. At that point she bent an earnest gaze on the blueberry patch, turning this way and that, and I believe selecting the very berry she desired; for she suddenly dropped like a shot, seized the berry, and was back on the post, as if the ground were hot. There she rested long enough for me to see what she held in her beak, and then disappeared in the silent way she had come. In a moment she returned; for it was not for herself she was berrying, but for some speckled-breasted beauty shyly hiding in the alder thicket below.

As the babies' month drew near its close, and August stood threateningly on the threshold, sometimes I heard young folk at their lessons. Most charming was a scion of the chewink family learning to ring his silver bell. I could not see him,—he was hidden behind the leafy screen across the river; but happily sounds are not so easily concealed as sights, and the little performance explained itself as clearly as if I had had the added testimony of my eyes (though I longed to see it, too). The instructor was a superior singer, such as I have heard but few times, and the song at its best is one of our most choice, consisting of two short notes followed by a tremolo perhaps an octave higher, in a loud clear ring like a silver-toned bell.

"Was never voice of ours could say
Our inmost in the sweetest way
Like yonder voice."

For several minutes this rich and inspiring song rang out from the bushes, to my great delight, when suddenly it ceased, and a weak voice piped up. It was neither so loud nor so clear; the introductory notes were given with uncertainty and hesitation, and the tremolo was a slow and very poor imitation. Still, it was plain that the towhee baby was practicing for his entrance into the ranks of our most bewitching singers. The next day, a chewink, I think the same whose music and whose teaching I had admired, honored me with a song and a sight together. He was as spruce as if he had just donned a new suit, his black hood like velvet, his chestnut of the richest, and his white of the whitest, and he sang from the top of a small pine-tree; sometimes, in the restless way of his family, scrambling over the branches, and again shifting his position to a small birch-tree.

INDIVIDUALITY OF FLOWERS.

Many other songs and singers I enjoyed in those pleasant mornings beside the river, till the hour for what Thoreau designates as "that whirlpool called a dinner" drew near, and then, unmindful of the philosopher's advice, I started slowly homeward, collecting as I went, materials to fill the vases in my room.

In gathering flowers, one needs to select with discretion, for they, no less than their winged neighbors in the pasture, have an individuality of their own. The wild rose, for example, is most amiable in lending itself to our enjoyment. Not only does it submit to being torn from the parental stem, but it will flourish perfectly, and go on opening bud after bud, so long as it has one to open, as lovely and as fragrant as its sisters on the bush. One needs only to snip off the heads whose petals have dropped, to have a fresh and beautiful bowl of roses every morning. The daisy too adorns our tables and our vases cheerfully, and as long as if it still stood among the grasses, its feet planted in mother earth; and even when it has lived out its allotted time, it neither withers nor droops, but begins to look wild, its petals losing their trim regularity and standing every way.

Different indeed is the disposition of the goldenrod, which, though remaining fresh and bright, when called upon to decorate our homes, obstinately refuses to open a petal after it is gathered; and the fairy-like elder, which sullenly resents being touched, gives up the struggle for existence and droops at once; and the cactus, which promptly draws its satin petals together, and stubbornly declines to open again. The loveliest bouquet of late July on the coast of Maine is this, which I give for the pleasure of other flower-lovers, if haply there be any who have not discovered it. Put in a vase a few stalks of completely opened goldenrod, of the variety that divides into long, finger-like stems. Let there be just enough so that when each blossom is spread out full they shall barely cover the space. Have the stems of equal length, so that the effect shall be flat, and not conical. Into this, between the blossoms, carefully stick the stems of a few fully spread lace flowers (or wild carrot), with stems two or three inches longer than you have allowed the goldenrod stems. Each must have full space to display every tiny floweret, and not to hide the golden glory beneath. When prepared, set the vase or bowl on the floor, before a grate or to light up some gloomy corner. Properly done the effect is a marvel and a joy forever, like lace over sunshine, like some fairy creation too dainty for words to picture.

IX.

DOWN THE MEADOW.

The bird-baby world was not bounded by any pasture, however enchanting, and I have not told all the charms of this one. The house where I found bed and board, in the intervals of bird study,—once a farmhouse, now an "inn of rest" for a country-loving-family,—was happily possessed of two attractions: the pasture toward which I turned with the morning sun, and a meadow which drew me when shadows grew long in the afternoon. This meadow began at the road passing in front of the house, and extended to the salt marsh which separated us from the sea. The marsh was always a beautiful picture,

"Stretching off in a pleasant plain
To the terminal blue of the main."

It was never twice the same, for it changed with every passing cloud, with every phase of the weather, with every tide; one never tired of it. And it was full of winged life: not only the beautiful gulls,

"Whose twinkling wings half lost amid the blue,"

in a white cloud over the far-off beach, but small birds of several kinds, who never came near enough to dry land to be identified. Sharp-tailed sparrows appeared on the meadow after grass was cut, and their exquisite ringing trill could always be heard from the bank; crows fed upon it every day; blackbirds' wings were always over it; and above all, sandpipers were there,

"Calling dear and sweet from cove to cove."

One afternoon, starting down the meadow on my usual visit to the sandpiper little folk, I heard a low cry of "flick-er! flick-er!" and there on the grass before me were two of the birds face to face. One was an adult, but the other was a nearly grown young one, and I saw in an instant that I had unwittingly intruded upon the breakfast he was about to receive. In the goldenwing family —as perhaps not every one knows—a repast is not over with one poke into an open bill; it is a far more serious affair indeed. The young bird opens his mouth a little, the parent thrusts his—or her—beak down the waiting throat, until one would think the infant must be choked, and then the elder delivers little pokes, as he crams down the mouthfuls, six, eight, even ten I have counted before he stops. Then the heads draw apart, and the grown-up—who has plainly come well provided—makes a sort of spasmodic movement in his own throat, probably raising from some internal reservoir another portion of

84

food, the infant opens his beak again, and the operation is repeated.

Of course my presence interfered with this elaborate, several-course breakfast, and the elder of the two fell to reproaching me by loud calls and vehement bows in my direction. Seeing that I was not sufficiently impressed, and did not depart, he resorted to stronger measures; he swayed his head from side to side, stretching out his neck like an enraged goose, and presenting a most droll appearance.

At first the youngster seemed to be paralyzed, but suddenly—perhaps realizing what harm my inopportune appearance had done—he also began to bow and sway, exactly as papa was doing. Anything more ludicrous than those two birds standing face to face and performing such antics it is hard to imagine; no one but a flicker could be at the same time so serious and so absurd.

At the edge of the meadow, where it sloped sharply down to the marsh, lived one whose days were full of trouble, which he took care to make known to the world,—a

> "Fire-winged blackbird, wearing on his shoulders
> Red, gold-edged epaulets."

His little family, not yet out of the nest, was settled safely enough behind a clump of bushes that fringed the marsh. But he, in his rôle of protector, had taken possession of two trees on the high land, where he could overlook the whole neighborhood, and see all the dangers, real and fancied, that might, could, would, or should threaten them, and "borrow trouble" to his heart's content. The trees, this bird's headquarters, were an aged and half-dead cherry and a scraggy and wind-battered elm, standing perhaps a hundred feet apart. On the top twig of one of these, or flying across between them, he was most of the time to be seen, and his various cries of distress, as well as his wild, woodsy song, came plainly up to me in my window.

The troubles of this Martha-like character began when mowers brought their clattering machine, and with rasping noise and confusion dire laid low the grass which had isolated him from the rest of the world, and that impertinent world poured in. First came crows, from their homes in the woods beyond the pasture, to feast on the numerous hoppers and crawlers left roofless by the mowers, and to procure food for their hungry young, and alighted in the stubble, two or three or half a dozen at a time. By this the soul of the redwing was fired, and with savage war-cries he descended upon them. His manner was to fly laboriously to a great height, and then swoop down at a crow as if to annihilate him. The bird on the ground turned from his insect hunt long enough to snap at his threatening enemy, and then returned to his serious business. So long as the crows stayed the redwing was frantic, his cries filled the air; and as they were almost constantly there, he was kept on the borders of frenzy most of the time.

After the crows came the bird-students, with opera-glasses and spying ways. These also the irascible redwing decided to be foes, flying about their heads threateningly, and never ceasing his doleful cries so long as they were in sight. I hoped his brown-streaked mate down in the marsh knew what a fussy and suspicious personage she had married, and would not be made anxious by his extravagances; but she too distrusted the bird gazers, adding her protests to his, and such an outpouring of "chacks" and other blackbird maledictions one—happily—is not often called upon to encounter.

After the bird-students the haymakers; and every time a man or a horse appeared in that field, the blackbird was thrown into utter despair, and the air rang with his lamentations.

He was evidently a character, a bird of individuality, and I was anxious to know him better; so, although I hated to grieve him, I resolved to go somewhat nearer, hoping that he would appreciate my harmlessness and soon see that he had nothing to fear from me. Not he! Having taken it into his obstinate little head that all who approached the sacred spot he guarded were on mischief bent, he refused to discriminate. The moment I approached the gate, the whole width of the meadow from him, he greeted me with shouts and cries, and did not cease for an instant, though I stayed two hours or more. I always went as modestly and inoffensively as possible through the meadow, far from his two trees, seated myself on the edge of the slope at some distance from him, and remained quiet. But he was never reconciled. His first act, as I started down the field, was to fly out to meet me, as if to drive me away. When he reached me, he would hold himself ten or fifteen feet above my head, perfectly motionless excepting a slight movement of the wings, looking as if he meditated an attack; and indeed I did sometimes fear that he would treat me as he did the crows. As I came nearer, his mate flew up out of the bushes, and added her demonstrations to his. Their movements in the air were beautiful. One would beat himself up quite high, and then hover, or apparently rest at that altitude, as if too light to come down, at last floating earthward, pausing now and then, as if he absolutely could not return to our level.

WHAT DID IT ALL MEAN?

Occasionally my presence caused a domestic scene not easy to interpret. Madam, no doubt fully aware of the prying ways of the human family, sometimes hesitated to return to her little ones in the bushes. She flew around uneasily, alighting here and there, anxious and worried, but plainly afraid of exposing her precious secret. Then her "lord and master" took her in hand, flying at her, and following wherever she fled before him, till he almost overtook her, when she dropped into the marsh, and with a low, satisfied chuckle he took a wide circle around and returned to his tree. Scolding all the time, she remained some minutes in the deep grass, then flew up high, and floated down to the alder clump where the nest was placed. Upon this, her observant lord, whose sharp eyes nothing escaped, instantly flew down again, dashed impetuously through the alders, and without pausing returned to his post. Now how should one interpret that little family interlude?

Later, when the young were out of the nest and quite expert on wing, the redwing's relations with them puzzled me also. I often saw the two who appeared to compose the family flying about with their mother, and I knew they were his because he frequently joined the party. But their conduct seemed unnatural, and a doubt stole over me whether this bird—this individual, I mean—could be a domestic tyrant. I knew from previous studies that the love-making manners of the redwing are a little on the "knock-down-and-drag-out" order of some savage tribes of our own species. To chase the beloved until she drops with fatigue seems to be the blackbird idea of a tender attention, and possibly the pursuit of his spouse already spoken of may have been of this sort, merely a loverly demonstration. But with the babies it was a different thing. Heretofore I had seen blackbird fathers devoted attendants on their young, working as hard as the mothers in seeking supplies, and following up the wandering brood to administer them. But this bird, I observed, was avoided by the little folk. When he showed inclination to join the family party on one of its excursions, they shied away from him, and if he came too near they uttered a sort of husky "huff," like the familiar protest of a cat. With the same sound they greeted him and moved away when he approached a bush where they sat. Perhaps this crustiness of demeanor was the natural result of his long weeks of anxiety and trouble as protector during their helpless infancy; perhaps he was tired out and exhausted, and it was not irritability, but nervous prostration, that made him appear so unamiable. Indeed, I do not see how it could be otherwise, after his exciting life. And may that not explain the fact that when the young are grown, the singer shakes off all family ties and joins a flock of his comrades, while mother and young remain together? Since he insists on taking his family responsibilities so hard, he cannot be blamed for desiring a rest for part of the year.

A PANIC ON THE MARSH.

Now that the nest was deserted and the young were always going about with their mother, I wondered that the head of the family did not relax his vigilance over the meadow and abandon his two watch-towers; but save that his enticing song came up to me oftener than his cries of distress, his habits were not materially altered. One day, when I thought his summer troubles ought surely to be over, a fresh anxiety came to him. Several women and girls, with a dog, appeared on the marsh, which at low tide was in some parts explorable. The human members of the party amused themselves with bathing and wading in the now shallow stream; but the dog acted like one·gone mad, dashing about on those peaceful flats where so many birds were enjoying themselves quietly, rushing full gallop from one group to another, wading or swimming the winding stream every time he came to it, and barking at the top of his voice every instant. Birds rose before him in flocks, sandpipers took to their wings in panic, swallows swooped down over him in anxious clouds, sharp-tailed sparrows and all other winged creatures fled wildly before this "agitator," who seemed to have no aim except to disturb, and reminded me irresistibly of his human prototype. Somewhere in that "league upon league of marsh grass," I suppose, were the blackbird's little folk; for the watcher on the bank was in deepest tribulation, and his outcries quickly brought me down to see what had happened.

The Young Americans of the redwing family are as vivacious and uneasy as might be expected of the scions of that house. No sooner do they get the use of their sturdy legs than they scramble out of the nest and start upon their bustling pilgrimage through life, first climbing over the bushes in their neighborhood, and as they learn the use of their wings becoming more venturesome, till at last, every time a hard-working mother brings a morsel of food, she has to hunt up her straggling offspring before she can dispose of it. Though eager for food as most youngsters, they are altogether too busy investigating this new and interesting world to stay two minutes in one place. So far from waiting, like Mr. Micawber, for something to turn up, they proceed, the moment they can use their limbs, to attack the problem of delay for themselves; to wait is not a blackbird possibility. It is needless to say that such preternaturally sharp and wide-awake Young Americans very soon graduate from the nursery.

A YELLOW-HEADED MONSTER.

The last trial that came to the blackbird, and the one, perhaps, that induced him finally to abandon his watch-towers and join his friends on the bank farther down, was the appearance one day in the meadow of a new importation from the city, a boy marked out for notice by a striking yellow-and-black cap. The instant he entered the inclosure afar off, the redwing uttered a shriek of hopeless despair, as who should say, "What horrible yellow-headed monster have we here?" and as long as he remained the bird cried and bewailed his fate and that of his family, as if murder and sudden death were the sure fate of them all. It was the last act in the blackbird drama on the meadow.

Between my morning in the pasture and my afternoon down the meadow, were two or three hours of rest beside my window, and there, too, the drama of life went on. On one side was an orchard—an orchard, alas! without bluebirds, for it was the summer following the dreadful tragedy in Florida, where thousands perished of hunger, and not one of the blue-coated darlings was to be seen where had always been many.

Perhaps, too, even more destructive than the death by hunger that year is the death which I am assured is common in all years about Washington, and doubtless other places; death at the hands of man—for the table. Who could eat a bluebird! It is bad enough to doom the bobolink to the pot after he has changed his coat and become a reedbird, and given some reason for his fate by his unfortunate fondness for rice. But what excuse can there be for bringing the "Darling of the Spring" to this woeful end?

To the deserted orchard came but one bird, a phœbe, and I believe his object was to retire from the world, for he was the most modest bird of his family that I ever saw. He dwelt in an obscure corner, and never so much as tried the peak of the barn, which was temptingly near. When he called it was almost in a whisper. I saw no indications that he had a nest or a family, and I am inclined to think that he was a misanthrope and a hermit.

A BIRD BABY SHOW.

Under my window on the other side came a vesper sparrow family. Three youngsters in bright new coats, quite unlike the worn and faded hues of their parents' dress. On the stone wall, or perched on a telegraph pole, close to the solitary insulator on the summit, the singer poured out his sweet little song, ending—in his best moods—in an exquisite trill that resembled the silver bell of the chewink. The family spent their time in the road or the meadow, the mother working hard to supply the hungry little mouths, which gave vent to queer whining cries. One day when it was raining the mother and one infant were out on the usual business, when suddenly they became aware of a chipmunk about eighteen inches from them, and at the same instant he saw them. He sat up very erect to look over the grass, and, holding his funny little hands over his heart, stared at the pair as if he had never seen birds. The baby sparrow flew a foot or two, but the elder ran toward him most valiantly, upon which the brave chipmunk took to his heels, scrambled up the stone wall, and disappeared.

Before the window, too, were always the swallows, for the telegraph wire was a favorite perch. And after the young were out, there was every day a baby show, the eave and tree swallows having adopted the wires as their out-of-door nursery. Nearly all the time might be seen half a dozen or more waiting patiently for a morsel from some of their elders circling about over their heads, and such a chatter as they kept up! They whispered softly among themselves when their parents were away, and called in squeaky little voices with fluttering wings as one of the elders approached. Whether the young in these social nurseries know their particular parents has always been an interesting question with me, and I studied their ways for some clew to the truth. I noticed when one of the parents swooped over them or came near, to alight, not more than one or two of the waiting babies on the wire would flutter and ask for food, and I saw also, on such occasions, that they were usually fed. When somewhat later another parent came near, a different little one would ask and be fed. They did not all, or even any great number, ask every time an old bird came about, which certainly looked as if the little ones knew their own parents.

After a while the swallows came out in great numbers. There were hundreds at a time on the telegraph wires, all, both old and young, talking at once—as it appeared. They had flight exercises, when the whole flock rose at once, filling the air with wings. This gathering continued for three or four days, while all other birds seemed to have disappeared, and then one morning they were gone to the marsh, where we often saw them afterward, and the other birds returned to their usual haunts.

X.

IN A COLORADO NOOK.

The loveliest nook I know is one of nature's wild gardens, on the banks of the "Shining Water," at the foot of the Rocky Mountains. It is forever fresh and green in my memory. Let me picture it for you, dear reader, as I saw it last.

It is June, and we are sitting under a low tree buried up to our shoulders in a luxuriant growth of weeds. Before us towers beautiful Cheyenne, its wonderful red rocks gorgeous in the morning sun; above us stretches the violet-blue sky, while all about us, filling our lungs, and bracing and invigorating our whole being, is the glorious mountain air of Colorado. Outside our shady nook the sunshine glows and burns, but we are cool and comfortable.

The little field between our seat and the mountain is all given up to weeds, with here and there a small oak-tree, and shut in by a hedge of oak saplings and low willows. I say weeds, but think not of an eastern weed-grown spot; imagine neither pigweed, smartweed, burdock, nor sorrel. Rather, picture in your mind a flower-bed, more rich and gay than ever met your admiring eyes. Yellow daisies by thousands turning their shining faces up to the sun; royal purple clusters of a blossoming mint glowing in the brilliant light; larkspurs four feet high, thrusting themselves above the rest like blue banners here and there; while lower down peep out white, and blue, and lavender, and other modest posies, and everywhere our familiar woods flower the wild geranium, whose office it seems to be in Colorado to fill all vacancies, much larger and more luxurious than ours, though quite as dainty and as impatient of handling. Almost within reach of our hand we easily count a dozen varieties of blossoms, while at the back of the little field are masses of a tall plant gone to seed. This departed bloom must have resembled our elder in shape and size, and now it makes a wonderful display of seeds in all shades of green, yellow, and golden brown, according to the various degrees of ripeness. It is very effective, almost more beautiful than blossoms, certainly more harmonious.

Over all this growing glory butterflies flutter, and bees go hither and thither, and still higher zigzag dozens of dragonflies. Behind us, a few steps away, is the brook Minnelowan, whose musical murmur is in our ears, but we will not turn around just yet. Truly it is good to be here; to rest from the world of conventionality; to get into harmony with nature; to steep our souls in the wildness, the freshness, and the eternal youth of the growing world about us.

But we are seeking birds; we must control our enthusiasm and listen. Now we become aware of low, sharp, insect-like cries about us. They seem to come from all sides at once; we find it impossible to locate them, till a sudden chorus of loud and excited "smacks" directs our attention to the tree over our heads, and our eyes fall upon a pair of frantic little fellow-creatures in golden yellow, hopping about on the branches, posturing and gesticulating with vehemence, and addressing their remarks most pointedly to us.

We have doubtlessly invaded what they consider their domain. Those insect-like chirps are the voices of their little folk, probably just out of the nest, brand-new, ignorant, and curious babies, who know no better than to stare at us, and make their comments within reach of our hands. They are not yet trained to know and avoid their greatest enemy, which you may not know, dear reader, that you are, not because you are bloodthirsty, but because you belong to a bloodthirsty race.

Now one of the babies comes in sight, in soft olive, with golden suggestions on tail and body; but mamma, horrified that he has exposed himself to our gaze, hurries him away, and soon the chorus of peeps and smacks—the yellow-bird baby talk—grows more distant, and the whole family of golden warblers is gone. It is remarkable how much these little folk know about our ways. If we walk through their territory talking and laughing, the birds will continue their own affairs, singing and calling, and carrying on their domestic concerns as though we were blind and deaf, as indeed most of us are to the abundant life about us. But when they see us quiet, looking at them, showing interest in their ways, they recognize us at once as a suspicious variety of the *genus homo*, who must be watched. At once they are on guard; they turn shy and try to slip out behind a bush, or—if hampered by an untrained family of little ones—attempt to expostulate with us, or to drive us away.

All this time you have perhaps been conscious of a delicate little song, like the ringing of a silver bell, over at the edge of our wild garden. Now listen; you will hear a rustle as of dead leaves, a low utterance like a hoarse "mew," then an instant's pause, and the bell song again. Turn your glass toward the thick shrubbery, at a point where you can see the ground at the foot of the bushes. In a moment you catch a glimpse of the mysterious bell-ringer, nearly as big as a robin, modestly dressed in black and white and chestnut, going about very busily on the ground; now giving a little jump that throws a light shower of dirt and leaves into the air, then looking earnestly in the spot thus uncovered, perhaps picking something up, then hopping to the lowest twig of the bush, and flinging out upon the air his joyous song. We are fortunate to see him so soon; he might tantalize us all day with his song, and never give us a glimpse of himself, for he delights in these quiet places, under the thickest shrubs. He is the towhee bunting or chewink, sometimes called ground robin, and in that corner of Colorado he takes the place the robin fills with us, the most common bird about the house.

Keep very still, and we may perhaps hear his most ecstatic song, for remember it is June, the wooing and nesting time of our feathered friends, when their songs and their plumes are in perfection. The love-song of this particular chewink is simply his usual silver-bell peal, with the addition of two rich notes in tremolo; first a note lower in the scale than the bell, then a note higher, each a soft, delicious, rapturous utterance impossible to describe, but enchanting to hear.

The nest is doubtless close by, but it will be lost time to hunt for it in a wilderness of bushes like this, for it is a mere cup in the ground, hidden under the thickest shrubs that the brown-clad spouse of the towhee can find. If we did uncover it we might not recognize it, so perfectly do the colors of the birds, old and young, and even of the eggs, harmonize with the earth in which it is placed.

I once found, in another place a nest full of chewink babies. It was where a patch of sage bushes stretched down the mountain, bordered by a thick clump of oak brush seven or eight feet high. My attention was called to it by the owner himself, who alighted on the oaks with a beak full of food, and at once began to utter his cry of distress, or warning to his mate. The moment he began I heard a rustle of wings behind me, and turning quickly had a glimpse of the shy dame, skulking around a sage bush. A little search revealed the nest, carefully hidden under the largest branch of the shrub. It was a deep cup, sunk into the ground to the brim, and three young birds opened their months to be fed when I parted the leaves above them.

Studying a nest among the sage bushes is not so easy as one might imagine. This was so closely covered by the low-growing branches that I could see it only by holding them one side. Moreover the sage is what is called in the books a social plant; where there is one there may be a thousand, as like each other as so, many peas. The particular bush that hid my chewink babies had to be marked, as one would mark the special tuft of grass that hides a bobolink's nest.

AMONG THE SAGE BUSHES.

However, I spent an hour or two every day in the sage patch, watching the wind sweep over it in silvery waves, and getting acquainted with the nesting-birds. All sorts of manœuvres the father of the family tried on me, such as going about carrying food conspicuously in the mouth, then pretending to visit a far-off spot and returning without it; but he always ended by mounting the oak brush, ruffling up his neck feathers till they stood out like a ruff, and uttering his cry; it can hardly be called of distress, it became so evidently perfunctory. His mate never tried deception, but relied upon skulking to and fro, unseen among the bushes.

In seven or eight days, as soon, in fact, as they could stand, the nestlings deserted the little home and I saw them no more, but I learned one fact new to me about the singing of the chewink. After the nest was abandoned I sat down in the usual place, hoping to hear the silver tremolo I am so fond of. In a moment my bird began. Securely hidden, as he thought, by the impenetrable oak brush, in the dim seclusion he loves, he poured out his simple yet effective song for some time. Then, to my amazement, with hardly a pause, he began a second song, quite different, and unlike any chewink song I have heard. I had thought this bird more closely confined to one rôle than most others, for none who have studied birds will agree with the poet that

"Each sings its word or its phrase, and then
It has nothing further to sing or to say;"

but I learned on this day, and confirmed it somewhat later, that the chewink can vary his song considerably.

But let us return to our nook. We will now turn around, and the world is totally changed for us. Let us seat ourselves under a tall old pine-tree, whose delicious aroma the hot sun draws out, and the gentle breeze wafts down to refresh and delight us here below.

Before us is the brook, faint-hearted in manner, and only a murmur where last summer it was a roar. Alas! the beautiful stream has seen reverses since first I lingered on its banks with joy and admiration. Far up above, just after it leaves the rocky walls of Cheyenne Cañon, it has fallen into the greedy hands of men who have drawn off half of it for their private service. So the sparkling waters which gathered themselves together near the top of Cheyenne, leaped gayly down the seven steps of the falls, and rushed and bounded over the rocks of the cañon, now run tamely down between rows of turnips and potatoes, water an alfalfa field, bathe the roots of a row of tired-looking trees, or put a lawn a-soak. The fragment that is left winds on its old way, not half filling its bed, with a subdued babble, suited to its altered fortunes.

A BEWITCHING BEAUTY.

Still there is enough to delight a brook-lover, and this spot is the chosen home of the most bewitching little beauty in all Colorado, the Arkansas goldfinch. Clumsy name enough for a tiny sprite of a birdling, not so large as our charming little goldfinch in his black cap. He is exquisite in olive green, with golden yellow breast, and the black cap and wings of his family, and he is most winsome in manner, with every tone in his varied utterances musical and delicious to hear. As he flies over in bounding waves, calling "Swe-eet! swe-eet!" often ending with an entrancing tremolo, your very soul is taken captive. What would you not give to see the dainty cradle of his younglings! Not far away you may see two thistle-blooms pulled to pieces; no doubt the down has gone to make a bed for goldfinch babies, for nothing that grows, except thistledown, is quite soft and delicate enough for the purpose.

We will not try to find the nest. He is the most shy, the most elusive of birds, living in the tops of the tallest trees, and flitting from one to another like a sunbeam, showing only a glint of a golden breast as he goes. One is maddened by the medley of calls and scraps of song, the trills and tremolos in the sweetest and most enticing tones, while not able to catch so much as a glimpse of the bonny bird who utters them. His love-song is utterly captivating, as rapturous as that of the American goldfinch, with a touch of plaintiveness that makes it wonderfully thrilling. It is mostly in tremolo, a sort of indescribable vocal "shake" that is enchanting beyond the power of words to express. When he is not singing, one may often hear his low, earnest chatter and talk with his mate, in the same plaintive and winsome tones.

Ah, how little we can see of what goes on about us, though we are closely watching, and every sense is alert! On one side is a flash of wings, and somebody disappears before he is seen; from the other comes an unfamiliar note, and a rustle of leaves, behind which the author is hidden. Here two bird voices are heard in excited talk, but your hasty glance falls only on the swaying twig that proclaims their flight; and in the tops of tall trees is a whole world of life and action entirely beyond your vision.

HOW TO BE HAPPY.

Early in the study of bird-life one must learn to be content with comparatively little, and not set his heart on solving every mystery of sound or glimpse which comes to him. One must be content to let some things remain unknown, and enjoy what he can understand, if he would be happy with nature. And if at some future time—as often happens—the mystery is solved, the joy is great enough to pay for waiting, and much greater than if he had worried and tramped the country over in attempts to settle it.

I have seen it recommended as the best way to know birds, to follow every note heard, till the bird is found and identified. This method requires great activity, and often an hour's search results in the discovery of an unfamiliar note of a familiar bird,—the robin or sparrow, perhaps. Meanwhile one has missed a dozen charming scenes in bird-life, and a chance to make acquaintances worth more than the gratification of that curiosity. The wiser course, it seems to me, is to learn to be content with what comes to you, and not mourn over what eludes you; to be happy with what nature offers you, nor make yourself miserable over what she for the present withholds; to adopt for your motto the grand words of a fellow bird-lover,—

"What is mine shall know my face."

And in spite of such regrets, enough is always left to repay patient waiting. From across the brook comes the unceasing cry of the Maryland yellow-throat, "Witches here! witches here!" and you can readily believe him, especially as with your best efforts you can see scarcely more than a suggestion of his quaint black mask, as a small form dives into the thick bushes.

Nor are birds the only attraction in this most fascinating nook; there are flowers. Through the dead pine leaves on which we sit, here and there thrusts itself up a slender stem, holding upright one of Colorado's matchless blossoms. This is the chosen nook of the rare gilia, which hides itself under the edge of a bush, or close against a low tree, bearing its pink and coral treasures modestly out of sight, until a flower-seeking eye spies it, glowing like a gem in the green world about it. Under the shrubs which hem in our nook on one side grows here and there a rosy cyclamen; out in the sunshine are bunches of bluebells; down the bank beside the water are great masses of golden columbine, while a fragrant veil of blooming clematis is flung over the weeds between. It is a rarely lovely and flowery spot.

SAUCY LITTLE WRENS.

We are not far from the world, however; this cañon-like valley of the Minnelowan is narrow, and through it passes the road. Moreover, there are many openings that might reveal us to the procession of tourists on their way up the cañon. But happily the sun is on our side, and the sun of Colorado is not to be despised: a screen of umbrellas and parasols and carriage curtains shuts us from view as completely as if the passers-by had no eyes on that side. If seen, we should be classed among the "sights," and the legitimate prey of the sight seeker. We should certainly be stared at, perhaps have glasses turned upon us, possibly be kodaked, and without doubt take prominent place in all the newspaper letters that go from here. But we may be sure of solitude till the sun crosses the road.

Yet this is far from solitude. Here comes a whole bevy reviling us, six or seven of them, running up and down the branches of a great bush, all scolding at the top of their voices,—a family of house wrens lately emancipated from their wooden castle in that old stump across the brook,—pert and saucy little parents, and droll babies imitating them with spirit.

The wrens were not the only tenants of that old tree-trunk; I have spent many hours beside it. Such conveniences for bird homes are rare in this country, and that one was well occupied, and offered a problem I was never able to solve. Beside the deserted woodpecker home to which the wrens had succeeded, there were two freshly made woodpecker doors, and both led to homes of the red-shafted woodpecker or western flicker, who differs from our familiar flicker only in having red instead of yellow shafts to his wing and tail feathers, and wearing the red badge of his family on his "mustaches" instead of on his collar, as does our bird.

One day when I was watching the stump, a male flicker came with food, and alighted at the lower door, upon which a young bird put his bill out and was fed in the murderous-looking fashion of the flickers. Papa thrust his long beak down baby's throat, and gave several vicious-looking pokes, as if to hammer something down. While I was musing over this strange way of feeding, the bird left, and a female flicker appeared. She glanced into the open door, and then to my surprise slipped half around the trunk and a foot higher, and stopped before the other hole, which I had not noticed till then. Instantly a head came out, much bigger than the first one, uttered the familiar flicker baby-cry, and was fed.

Then the question that interested me was, Were there two nests, or one of two stories with babies of different ages? Did both belong to one pair, or was that little dame peeping into her neighbor's house? Much time I spent before that castle in the air, but never was able to answer my own questions. No two old birds came at the same time, and no difference could I discover in looks or manners, that answered the query whether there were one or two pairs at work. Now they have all flown, and only the laugh of the flicker and the call of the young ones all around remain to tell that woodpecker babies grew up in the tree.

THE GLORY OF THE WEST.

Now let us close our glasses, fold our camp-chairs, and go back to the camp, our present home. As we turn into the gate another voice strikes our ear, louder, richer, more attention-compelling than any we have heard. Listen: It is the wonder and the glory of the West; it is the most intoxicating, the most soul-stirring of bird voices in the land where thrushes are absent; it embodies the solitude, the vastness, the mystery of the mesa; it is the western meadow lark. This is his nesting-time, and we may be treated to his love-song, the exquisite, whispered aria he addresses to his mate. As I have heard it when very close to him, he sings his common strain several times, and then drops to a very low twittering and trilling warble, in which now and then is interpolated a note or two of the usual score, yet the whole altogether different in spirit and execution. He ends by a burst into the loud carol he offers to the world. There is nothing beyond that to hear, even in my beloved nook.

XI.

THE IDYL OF AN EMPTY LOT.

A CITY STUDY.

Opposite my study windows is an empty lot. It is of generous size; six residences facing another street, with high board fences, stretch across the back; a large apartment-house towers above it on the right, and a tight fence defines it on the left. The front is open to the street, but the whole is so given up to weeds, such a tangle of rank vegetation, that few people penetrate it, and it is the great out-of-doors for the animal life of the neighborhood. Looking down upon it as I do, constantly spread out under my windows, I cannot choose but see everything that goes on.

Last summer was the blossoming-time of the empty lot. It had but one summer of romance—just one—between the building of the brick row behind it and the beginning of the new row which shall hide it from the sun for ages, perhaps.

A RELAPSE INTO BARBARISM.

It was not attractive in the spring, for man had done what he could to deface it. Here is a curious fact: the human being is capable of a certain amount of civilization under the pressure of the necessities of city life. He—or she—will learn to dispose inoffensively of the waste and rubbish that drag after him like a trail wherever he goes. He—and always likewise she—can be taught to burn his waste paper, to bag his rags, to barrel his ashes, to burn the refuse from his table, to hide the relics of china and glass. In fact, he *can* live in a modern house with no back yard, no "glory-hole" whatever.

Yet if one would see how superficial his culture, how easy his relapse into barbarism, he need only open his windows upon an empty lot. This tempting space, this unguarded bit of the universe, brings out all the savage within him. Ashes and old boots, broken glass, worn-out tin pans, and newspapers whose moment is over, alike drift naturally into that unfortunate spot. The lot under my window had suffered at the hands of lawless men,—not to say women,—for it offered the eternal oblivion of "over the back fence" to no less than ten kitchens with their presiding genii.

Nor was this all. The lot and all the land about it had belonged to an unsettled estate, and for years had been a dumping-ground for carts, long before the surrounding buildings had begun their additions to its stores.

99

But last spring a change came to it. Its nearly fenced condition for the first time allowed Mother Nature a chance, and anxious, like other mothers, to hide the evil deeds of her children, she went busily to work,

"With a hand of healing to cover the wounds
   And strew the artificial mounds
And cuttings with underwood and flowers."

We may call them weeds, but forever blessed be the hardy, rapid-growing, ever-ready plants we name so scornfully! What else could so quickly answer the mother's purpose? She had not time to evolve a century-plant, or elaborate an oak-tree, before man would be upon it again. She did the best she could, and the result was wonderful.

When I returned from the country I found, to my delight, in place of the abomination of desolation I have described, a beautiful green oasis in the world of stone and brick. From fence to fence flourished and waved in the breeze an unbroken forest. The unsightly heaps had become a range of hills, sloping gently down to the level on one side, and ending on the other in an abrupt declivity, with the highest peak bare and rocky, overhanging a deep and narrow ravine. The bordering fences were veiled by luxurious ailanthus shoots, chicory blossoms opened their sweet blue eyes to every morning sun, and it was beside

"Rich in wild grasses numberless, and flowers
Unnamed save in mute Nature's inventory."

In the air above, myriads of dainty white butterflies sported, ever rising in little agitated parties of two or three, climbing gayly the invisible staircase till at an immense height, and then fluttering back to earth no wiser than they went up, so far as the human eye could see.

The forest, as I have called it, was, to be sure, by measurement of man, not more than three or four feet high. But all things are relative, and to the frequenters of that pleasant bit of woodland, far above whose head it towered, it was as the deep woods to us. I chose to look at it from their point of view, and to them it was a noble forest, resembling indeed a tropical jungle, so thickly grown that paths were made under it, where might be enjoyed leisurely walks, given up to quiet and meditation. For there were inhabitants in plenty,—the regulars, the transients, the stragglers,—in furs, in feathers, in wings.

In this nook, secluded from the world which every day swept by without a glance, a constant drama of life went on, which I could see and be myself unseen. I soon became absorbed in the study of it. The actors were of that mysterious race which lives with us, and yet is rarely of us; whose real life is to us mostly a sealed book, and of whom Wordsworth delightfully sings,—

> "Think of the beautiful gliding form,
> The tread that would scarcely crush a worm,
> And the soothing song by the winter fire
> Soft as the dying throb of the lyre."

Yes, the cats, whose ways are ever the unexpected, and of whom I am so fond that one of the most touching objects unearthed at Pompeii—to me—is the skeleton of a woman holding in her arms the skeleton of a cat, whom perhaps she gave her life to save.

The builder of the fences at the back of this Cat's Eden very considerately capped them all with a board three inches wide, thus making a highway for the feline race, not only across the back, but from that to each house door. On this private path, above the heads of boys and dogs, they spent much time. This was their Broadway, and at the same time their point of outlook, where they might survey the landscape and decide when and where to enter their secluded domain. How admirable the facility with which these mysterious beasts pass up or down high fences! Ladders or stairs are superfluous. How can one possibly walk several steps down a perpendicular board without falling headlong to the ground? And still more strange,—how can one leap squarely against the same fence, and run right up to the top?

THREE REGULARS.

101

Soon after breakfast on every fair day the houses around began to give up their cats. There were three in whose actions I became specially interested. The most important, and the one to whom I felt the place belonged by right of appreciating it, was a personage of dignified manners, and evidently of rank in his own world, a magnificent silver tabby, the beauty of the neighborhood. Next in interest was a white-and-black cat for whom I had sincere respect because she lived most amicably with two canaries whose cages were always within reach and never disturbed. The third was to my eyes anything but attractive, being a faded-looking gray tabby, who entered the place by a hole under the fence next the apartment-house. She looked ill-used, as if her home life was troubled by bad children, or a frivolous, teasing dog, or a raging housekeeper who left no peace to man or beast.

For whatever cause, when, soon after breakfast, Madam Grey appeared on the scene, she proceeded at once and in silence to the highest bare peak of the hills, a sightly place where she could overlook the thick green forest, with its shady walks and cool retreats, and have timely notice of any approach from the street. On that point she found or made a slight depression, and there she calmly dressed her fur, and then, wrapping her robe around her (so to speak), slept hours at a time.

She never did anything on the lot except sleep, and she seemed totally blind to the attractions of nature. I never saw her notice anything. As soon as she awoke she went back through the humble portal to her flat.

This piece of woods was not merely a pleasure-ground. It was a hunting-field as well, and the denizens of its quiet shades were not at all averse to a little excitement of the chase, nor to a taste now and then of wild game of their own catching. What was there I know not, but I judge from the spasmodic character of the hunt that it was grasshoppers.

The silver tabby and the white-and-black, who were daily visitors to the place, never quarreled with each other, and their intercourse, when they happened to meet on the common highway, was conducted in the courteous and dignified manner of the race.

Cats are popularly supposed to dislike wet, but I have seen two of them in a steady rain conduct an interview with all the gravity and deliberation for which these affairs are celebrated. The slow approach, with frequent pauses to sit down and meditate, or "view the landscape o'er," the earnest and musical —if melancholy—exchange of salutations, the almost imperceptible drawing nearer, with the slightly waving tail the only sign of excitement, and at last the instantaneous dash, the slap or scratch (so rapid one can never tell which), the fiery expletive and retort, and the instant retreat, to sit down again. There seems to be some canon of feline etiquette which forbids two to meet and pass without solemn formalities of this sort, reminding one of the ceremonious greetings of the Orient, where time is of no particular value.

A WAY OF HIS OWN.

The silver tabby was an original, and had a way of his own. He seemed impatient of these serious rites, and when within three feet of his *vis-à-vis* he usually gave one great leap over the intervening space, administered his salute,—whatever it was,—and passed on. This cat was peculiar in other ways. Sometimes he had the whole wood to himself, and it was charming to see him wander in his leisurely way all over it, smelling daintily of this and that, now tasting a leaf, now looking intently at some creeper or crawler on the ground, now sitting down to enjoy the seclusion and the silence of the wood. He was a philosopher, or a lover of nature,

"A lover who knows by heart
Each joy the mountain dales impart."

One of the accusations brought against this reserved little beast is that he does not love man. Has he reason to do so? Tragedies I have seen on the lot, which I try to forget and shall not repeat, in which small boys demonstrated in their treatment of the abused race how much more brutal than a brute the human animal can be. Cats show their intelligence by being wary of mankind.

When October at last stripped the woods of their summer glory, and the weather was no longer warm, the heat-loving creatures deserted the empty lot, except the silver tabby, who often came out and sauntered through its lonely paths, smelling of the weeds here and there, seating himself in a bower that was still green, rubbing his face against something he found there, and evidently enjoying sufficient society in his own thoughts, for to him plainly it was still

"A woodland enchanted."

Then came a week of unwonted glory, of distinguished visitors. All the summer birds had hovered over it; toward evening the night hawk circled high in air above it, uttering his wild, quaint cry, collecting food for his little family, no doubt safely reposing on some gravel roof near by.

A RARE VISITOR.

And there were always the city sparrows. They had taken possession of a vine, which, clambering up the back of one of the houses bordering the lot, had burst into sudden luxuriance when it found itself without further support at the eaves, spreading out each side, and clinging for dear life to the roof, making a delightful screen, as well as a comfortable site for many bird homes. Indeed, there seemed to be a populous bird village behind the green curtain, and great disturbances sometimes occurred, and I could hear the excited voices of the residents till darkness put an end to their discussions. One cool October day, as I sat at my window I heard a strange bird note, and my ready glass in a moment revealed a rare visitor indeed,—a thrasher. He stood on the edge of a roof silhouetted against the sky, tossing his tail in excitement, and peering eagerly into the yards opened out before him. Suddenly he dashed into a tall rosebush leaning on the back fence of the empty lot, and busied himself a few moments, perhaps with the rose hips; then finding that too near the four-footed inhabitants, he retired to the roof, looked to see that no plebeian sparrows were at home in the vine, then plunged into that and disappeared behind its ample foliage. Here he spent some time getting the berries, as I could see, and during his occupancy no sparrow entered, though some flew by. All day he remained in the vicinity; but at night I suppose he resumed his journey southward, for I saw him no more.

One day a pair of juncos appeared on the scene, mingling fraternally with the sparrows, and sharing their usual pickings around back doors and along the back fence, and white-throated sparrows showed themselves on the shrubs and small trees which overhung the division walls.

But the crowning day of the empty lot came still later, when a fairy-like kinglet hunted over the rosebushes, and that shy woods dweller, the hermit thrush, condescended to show his graceful form on the fence, until the silver tabby, seeming to regard their calls as intrusions, took up his station on the cats' highway and I saw the birds no more.

IN THE BIRD-ROOM.

XII.

THE SOLITAIRE.

Give sunlight for the lark and robin,
    Sun and sky, and mead and bloom;
But give for this rare throat to throb in,
And this lonesome soul to sob in,
    Wildwoods with their green and gloom.

COATES KINNEY.

For three years there lived in my house one of the remarkable birds described in their native land as "invisible, mysterious birds with the heavenly song." I have hesitated to write of him, because I feel unable to do justice either to himself or to his musical abilities; and, moreover, I am certain that what I must say will appear extravagant. Yet when I find grave scientific books indulging in a mild rapture over him; when learned travelers, unsuspected of sentimentality or exaggeration, rave over him; when the literary man, studying the customs, the history, and the government of a nation, goes out of his way to eulogize the song of this bird, I take heart, and dare try to tell of the wonderful song and the life no less noble and beautiful.

Among eight or ten American birds of as many kinds, the solitaire, or, as he is called, the clarin, reminds one of a person of high degree among the common herd. This may sound absurd; but such is the reserve of his manner, the dignity of his bearing, the mystery of his utterances, and the unapproachable beauty of his song, that the comparison is irresistible. The mockingbird is a joyous, rollicking, marvelous songster; the wood thrush moves the very soul with his ecstatic notes; the clarin equals the latter in quality, with a much larger variety. He is an artist of the highest order; he is "God's poet," if any bird deserves the name; he strikes the listener dumb, and transports him with delight.

The solitaires, *Myadestes*, or fly-catching thrushes, are natives of the West Indies and Mexico, with one branch in the Rocky Mountains. My bird was *M. obscurus*, and came from Mexico. I found him in a New York bird-store, where he looked about as much at home among the shrieking and singing mob of parrots and canaries as a poet among a howling rabble of the "great unwashed."

NO DESIRE TO LIVE.

Upon a casual glance he might be mistaken for a catbird, being about his size, with plumage of the same shade of dark slate, with darker wings and tail and slightly lighter breast; but a moment's examination showed his great difference from that interesting bird. His short, sharp, and wide beak indicated the flycatcher, and his calm dark eyes were surrounded with delicate lines of minute white feathers, a break at each corner just preventing their being perfect rings.

Being a warm admirer of the catbird, I noticed the stranger first for the resemblance; but a few moments' study of his look and manner drew me strongly to himself, and though I desired only our native birds, I could not resist him.

When introduced to his new quarters in my house, the clarin did not flutter; he did not resist. He rested on the bottom of the cage where he was placed, and looked at me with eyes that said, "What are *you* going to do with me?" He had already accepted his imprisonment; he did not expect to be free, and it was plain that he no longer cared for his life. If he were to be subjected to the indignity of traveling in a box among common birds, as he had been sent from the bird-store where I found him, he had no desire to live. It required much coaxing to make him forget the outrage, and I am glad to say it was the last affront he suffered. From that day he was treated as lie deserved, being always at liberty in the room, and enjoying the distinguished consideration of a houseful of people and birds. Before he came to understand that his life had changed, however, I feared he would die. He did not mope, he simply cared for nothing. For more than twenty-four hours he crouched on the floor of his cage, utterly indifferent even to a comfortable position; food he would not look at. I talked to him; I screened him from noisy neighbors; I made his cage attractive; I spared no effort to win him,—and at last I succeeded. He took up again the burden of life, hopped upon a perch, and began to dress his feathers. Soon he was induced to eat, and then he began to notice the bird voices about him. Like other of the more intelligent birds, once won, he was entirely won. He was never in the least wild with me after that experience; never hesitated to put himself completely in my power, or to avail himself of my help if he needed it in any way. Says another bird-lover, "Let but a bird—that being so free and uncontrolled—be willing to draw near and conclude a friendship with you, and lo, how your heart is moved!"

A MYSTICAL CALL.

It is hard to tell in what way this bird impressed every one with a sense of his imperial character, but it is true that he did. He never associated with the other birds, and he selected for his perches those in the darker part of the room, where his fellows did not go. Favorite resting-places were the edge of a hanging map, the top of a gas fixture, and a perch so near my seat that most birds were shy of it. Though extravagantly fond of water, requiring his bath daily, he greatly disliked to bathe in the dishes common to all. Like a royal personage, he preferred his bath in his own quarters.

Moreover, the clarin never added his voice to a medley of music. If moved to sing while others were doing so, he first reduced them to silence by a peculiar mystical call, which had a marked effect not only upon every bird in the room, but upon the human listeners as well. This call cut into the ripple of sweet sounds about him like a knife, loud, sharp, and incisive, instantly silencing every bird. It consisted of two notes exactly one octave apart,—the lower one first,—uttered so nearly together that they produced the effect of one double note. After a pause of a few seconds it was repeated, as clear and distinct as before, with mouth open wide. It was delivered with the deliberation of a thrush; the bird standing motionless except the tail, which hung straight down, and emphasized every note with a slight jerk. This loud call, having been given perhaps twenty times, began to diminish in volume, with longer intervals between, till it became so faint it could scarcely be heard,—a mere murmur with closed bill, yet so remarkable and so effective that for some time not a bird peeped. Occasionally, while the room was quiet, he began to sing; but again it appeared that it was his purpose merely to hush the babble of music, for, having secured his beloved stillness, the beautiful bird remained a long time at rest, sitting closely on his perch, plainly in deep content and happiness. Sometimes, when out in the room, he delivered the call with extraordinary excitement, turning from side to side, posturing, flirting one wing or both, lifting them quite high and bringing them down sharply; but when in the cage at dusk—his favorite time—he stood, as I said, motionless and without agitation.

In another way my bird differed from nearly all the feathered folk, and proved his right to belong to the thrush family; he was not in any degree fussy; he never hopped about aimlessly, or to pass away time. He had not only a beautiful repose of manner, but there was an air of reticence in everything he did. Even in so trivial a matter as eating, he was peculiar. During the season he was always supplied with huckleberries, of which he was exceedingly fond. Any other bird would take his stand beside the dish, and eat till he was satisfied; but quite otherwise did the clarin. He went deliberately to the floor where they were, took one berry daintily in the tip of his beak, returned with it to the upper perch, fixed his eyes upon me, and suddenly, without a movement, let it slip down his throat, his eyes still upon me, with the most comically solemn expression of "Who says I swallowed a berry?" Then he stood with an air of defiant innocence, as if it were a crime to eat berries, not wiping his bill nor moving a feather till he wanted another berry, when he ate it in exactly the same way.

AT THE MIRROR.

The clarin defended himself against imposition, but, except to his own reflection in the glass, he never showed warlike inclinations. Upon his first sight of himself he was much excited. His feathers rose, especially on the back, where they looked like a hump; his beak pointed toward the offensive stranger, he uttered a peculiar new war-cry and then flung himself violently upon the enemy. Of course he brought up against the glass, and dropped panting to the bureau. In a moment he rallied, poured out a few unfamiliar notes in a loud strange voice, with wings quivering, body swaying from side to side, and tail wide spread. Then lifting both wings high above his back, he repeated the attack. Finding himself a second time baffled, he remained where he had dropped, silent, a picture of despair.

I hastened to end his trouble by covering the glass. He flew several times around the room, then alighted, reduced the inmates to meek silence by his mysterious calls, then flew to his own cage, retired to the upper perch, and remained quiet and motionless for an hour or more; apparently meditating upon the strange occurrence, and wondering how the elusive stranger had disappeared. During his trouble before the glass, all the birds in the room were excited; they always were close observers of everything he did, and never seemed to regard him as one of themselves.

In the spring, when the room was emptied of all its tenants excepting two or three who could not be set free, the clarin was a very happy bird. He flew freely and joyously about, delighting especially in sweeping just over my head as if he intended to alight, and he sang hours at a time. The only disturbance he had then—the crumpled roseleaf in his lot—was the presence of a saucy blue jay, a new-comer whom he could neither impress by his manner nor silence by his potent calls. So far from that, the jay plainly determined to outshriek him; and when no one was present to impose restraint on the naughty blue-coat (who, as a stranger, was for a time quite modest), he overpowered every effort of his beautiful *vis-à-vis* by whistles and squawks and cat-calls of the loudest and most plebeian sort. At the first sound of this vulgar tirade the imperial bird was silent, scorning to use his exquisite voice in so low company; while the jay, in no whit abashed, filled the room with the uproar till some one entered, when he instantly ceased.

WRAPPED IN FUSS.

The regularity of the clarin's bath has been mentioned; he dried himself, if possible, in the sunshine. Even in this he had his own way, which was to raise every feather on end; the delicate tips rose on his crown, the neck plumage stood out like a ruff, the tail spread, and the wings hung away from the body.

In this attitude, he looked as if wrapped in exquisite furs from his small beak to his slender black legs. He shared with all thrushes a strange restlessness on the approach of evening. First he moved back and forth on one perch with a gliding motion, his body crouched till the breast almost touched the perch, tail standing up, and wings quivering. Then he became quiet, and uttered his call for some time, and soon after settled for the night, sleeping well and even dreaming, as was evident from the muffled scraps of song and whispered calls that came from his cage.

This bird has all the sensitiveness of an artistic temperament, and one can readily believe that in freedom he would choose a life so secluded as to merit the popular name, "the invisible bird," inhabiting the wildest and most inaccessible spots on the rough mountain-side, as Mr. Frederic A. Ober found some of his near relations in the West Indies. If, in spite of his reserved manners, any bird was impertinent enough to chase or annoy him, he acted as if his feelings were hurt, went to his cage, and refused to leave it for some time. Yet it was not cowardice, for he could and did defend his cage against intruders, flying at them with cries of rage. Also, if his wishes chanced to interfere with the notions of another bird,—as they did on one or two occasions that I noticed,—he showed no lack of spirit in carrying them out. Once that I remember, he chose to perch on the top of a certain cage next a window, where he had not before cared to go. The particular spot that he occupied was the regular stand of another bird, one also accustomed to having his own way, and quite willing to fight for it,—a Brazilian cardinal. The cardinal, of course, disputed the point with the clarin, but the latter retained his position as long as he desired, running at the enemy with a cry if he ventured to alight near. In general, his tastes were so different from others that he seldom came into collision with them.

NOT DARING TO LAUGH.

When, on the approach of spring, some of his room-mates grew belligerent, and there arose occasional jarring between them, my bird showed his dislike of contention and coarse ways by declining to come out of his cage at all. Although the door stood open all day, and he was kept busy driving away visitors, he insisted on remaining a hermit till the restless birds were liberated, when he instantly resumed his usual habits, and came out as before. His sensitiveness was exhibited in another way,—mortification if an accident befell him. For example, when, by loss of feathers in moulting, he was unable to fly well, and fell to the floor instead of reaching the perch he aimed at, he stood as if stunned, motionless where he happened to drop, as if life were no longer worth living. Once he fell in this way upon a table beside a newspaper. As he landed, his feet slid on the polished surface, and he slipped partly under the loose paper, so that only his head appeared above it. There he stood for five minutes looking at me, and bearing a droll resemblance to a bird's head on a newspaper. He was not more than four feet from me, and was obviously deeply chagrined, and in doubt whether he would better ever try to recover himself; and I positively did not dare to laugh, lest I hurt him more.

The first time the clarin fell to the floor, I ventured to offer him the end of a perch which I held. Not in the least startled, he looked at it, then at me, then accepted the civility by stepping upon it, and holding there while I lifted and carried him to the door of the cage. This soon came to be the regular thing, and all through the trying season of moulting he waited for me to bring a perch and restore him to the upper regions where he belonged. He would have been easily tamed. Even with no efforts toward it, he came on my desk freely, talked to me, with quivering wings, and readily ate from my finger. The only show of excitement, as he made these successive advancements, was the rising of some part of his plumage. At one time he lifted the feathers around the base of his head, so that he appeared to have on a cap a little too big, with a fringe on the edge; and on his first alighting on the arm of the chair where I sat, the feathers over his ears stood out like ear-muffs.

IMITATING THE JAY.

When at last the clarin and the blue jay were left nearly alone in the room, I noticed that the clarin began watching with interest the movements of the jay. They had never come in collision, except of the voice above mentioned, because the jay preferred the floor, chairs, and desk, and seldom touched the perches, while the clarin nearly lived upon them. But after some study the latter clearly made up his mind to try the places his larger room-mate liked so well. He had already learned to go upon the desk and ask for currants, which in the absence of fresh berries I kept soaking in a little covered dish. If, after asking as plainly as eloquent looks and significant movements of wings could, I did not take the hint and give him some, he flew over my head, just touching it as he passed. But now, having resolved to imitate the jay, he went to the floor, and tried all of his chosen retreats: the lower rounds of the chair, my rockers, my knee, and the back of a chair sacred to the jay. During these excursions into unknown regions he discovered that warm air came out of the register, and apparently thinking he had discovered summer, he perched on the water-cup that hung before it, spread his feathers, and seemed as happy as if he had really found that genial season.

Who can describe the song of a bird? Poets and prose writers alike have lavished epithets on nightingale and mockingbird, wood thrush and veery, yet who, till he heard one, could imagine what its song was like? Yet I must speak of it.

Singing was always a serious matter with my bird; that is, he never sang while eating or flying about, interpolating his exquisite notes between two mouthfuls, or dropping them from the air. He always placed himself deliberately, and waited for the room to be still,—or made it so, as already related. During the first few months of his residence with me he gave one song of perhaps twenty notes, ending in a lovely tremolo. This had great variety of arrangement, but all bore unmistakable resemblance to the original theme. It was in quality totally unlike any bird note I ever heard, and thrilling in an extraordinary degree, though it was uttered with the beak nearly closed. I can readily believe what Mr. Ober and others assert, that it must have a startling effect when poured out freely in his native woods.

This song alone placed the clarin at the head of all songsters that I have heard or heard of, and I have heard all of our own best songsters, and the nightingale and wood lark of Europe. But after nearly a year of this he came out one memorable day with an entirely new melody, much more intricate and more beautiful, which for some time he reserved for very special and particular occasions, still giving the former one ordinarily. Some months later, to my amazement, he added a third chant, part of which so resembled that of the wood thrush that if he had been near one I should have thought it a remarkable mimicry. He delivered this with the exquisite feeling of the native bird, even the delicious quivering tone at the end, which indeed my bird often repeated in a low tone by itself. Sometimes, when the room was very still and he sitting on his perch, feathers puffed out, perfectly happy, he breathed out this most bewitching tremulous sound without opening his beak,—a performance enchanting beyond words to express.

AN ENCHANTING SINGER.

These themes the clarin constantly varied, and in the three years of his life with me I often noted down, in a sort of phonetic way, his songs, as he delivered them, and I have six or seven that are perfectly distinct and different. He never mixed them together or united them; he rarely sang two on the same day. All through, too, there seemed so much reserve power that one could not resist the conviction that he could go on and on, and break one's heart with his voice if he chose. The bird's own deep feeling was shown by his conduct; the least movement in the room would shut him up instantly. One could heartily say with another bird-lover across the sea, "If he has not a soul, who will answer to me for the human soul?"

It was reserved for the last weeks of his life for my bird to give me the most genuine surprise. One day I sat quietly at my desk. The bird stood on a perch very near my head,—so near I could not turn to look at him, when, without a moment's hesitation, without an instant's preliminary practice, he burst out into a glorious, heavenly, perfect song that struck me dumb and breathless. Not daring to move hand or foot, yet wanting some record of the wonderful aria, I jotted down, in the page I was writing, a few of the opening notes; I could re-write my page, but I could not bear to lose the music. Three times, at intervals of perhaps one minute, he uttered the same marvelous song, and then I never heard it again. After all, I had not a record of it, for though it was deliberate and distinct, at every repetition I was spellbound, and could not separate it into tones.

Though I should live to be a thousand years old, and visit every country under heaven, I am sure I should never hear such a rapturous burst of song again,—

> "Low and soft as the soothing fall
> Of the fountains of Eden; sweet as the call
> Of angels over the jasper wall
> That welcomes a soul to heaven."

After the foregoing study was written, Mr. Frederic A. Ober kindly placed at my disposal his unpublished notes upon another solitaire, the *siffleur montagne*, or mountain whistler. He had the bird in confinement for some time, while in the Antilles on a collecting tour for the United States National Museum; and the bird's character, as shown in captivity, so closely resembled the one I have tried to depict, that I give it as evidence that others have similarly interpreted the manners of the family.

LOVE OF SOLITUDE.

To begin with his love of solitude, one of the strongest characteristics of the *Myadestes* wherever found. It is that more than anything else which, in connection with his wonderful song, has wrapped the bird in mystery, and aroused the superstitions of the natives of the countries in which he lives. Mr. Ober says, and every one of the few observers who have succeeded in seeing the bird confirms the statement, that he is found only in the most solitary places, inaccessible mountains, wild, gloomy ravines, and dark, impenetrable gorges. Here the graceful bird delights to dwell, calling and singing from his post on a branch overhanging the perpendicular cliffs, hundreds of feet above the level earth. One of them, indeed, secures his beloved solitude by inhabiting the craters of extinct volcanoes.

In sprightliness of manner this bird of solitude reminds one of the catbird, whom he also greatly resembles in looks. He has the quick-darting movements of the flycatchers, and at the same time a strange, preoccupied air, that seems to make him oblivious of people, although they may be within a few feet of him.

Passing one of these peculiarly lonely places one day in his wanderings, Mr. Ober heard the note of the siffleur close at hand. He crept cautiously through the trees until he saw the bird, who had ceased singing, and was eating berries from a tall shrub, clinging to its hanging branches.

He soon finished his repast, flew to a dead branch, plumed his feathers, and after a few moments resumed his singing. He uttered a few trills of a rare musical quality that held his listener spellbound, then lightly flew to another branch overhanging the little ravine, at the bottom of which a babbling brook made music,—"not so liquid as siffleurs,"—says the historian. Here a few more strains fell from him, then he flitted to a swinging vine, repeated his bewitching note, and in a moment disappeared. The tones, says Mr. Ober, "are thrilling with solemn music and indescribably impressive." They have also a ventriloquial quality, and many tunes had he vainly searched for the singer, until a note of another sort betrayed his position, which was sometimes almost over the observer's head.

One morning a captive siffleur was dragged out of the trousers pocket of one of his "ragged brigade" and presented to the chronicler. These boys, whose help was indispensable to the collector, were a study in themselves. They were familiar with the habits, songs, and food of every bird in the woods, as well as expert in imitating the note of each one, and by this means drawing him to the fatal limed twigs. The interesting birds of the mountains, the siffleur, the trembleur, and others, they attracted by a peculiar hissing noise.

THE BIRD INSULTED.

The bird brought to Mr. Ober had been caught by bird-lime and was unhurt, but greatly mortified and insulted by his treatment. He seemed at first dazed, and utterly silent. But after a while he gave utterance to a cry of distress, which he repeated at intervals on that first morning, particularly when people came too near him. Before night he evidently realized the uselessness of protests, and became silent. He never for a moment displayed the wild terror and panic seen in most birds when first caught.

The next morning he ate berries and drank fresh water calmly and without fear; but for several days he did not utter a sound. One of the peculiarities of these birds is their fearlessness in the presence of man, or perhaps more correctly their intelligence, which prevents them, as it does our native thrushes, from being frightened unless there is something really alarming.

This is the natural and charming attitude of bird and beast toward man, until taught by deadly experience what they have to dread, as has been proved many times.

It is not, therefore, in the case of the solitaires, fear of man which drives them to their secluded dwelling-places. It is a certain reserve of character, a strong dislike to a crowd, a genuine love of solitude, and who shall say there is not also an appreciation of the attractions of scenery!

After Mr. Ober's bird had become used to his captivity, the collecting boys brought in another prisoner, a trembleur, so named because of his curious and restless manners, the jerks and quivers, the spasmodic movements of head and wings and tail, and the bows and postures with which he does everything.

The unfortunate trembleur indulged in no amusing antics on this occasion, however. He was overwhelmed by the extent of the disaster that had befallen him,—captivity in the hands of his worst foe. He crouched in one corner of his box, looking with wonder at his surroundings.

Now appeared a new trait in the character of siffleur. His deep love of solitude was even aggressive; he would not tolerate the intrusion of another bird upon his domain. He greeted his fellow-sufferer first with hisses and then with threats and feints of war. Trembleur did not respond, but he presented his formidable bill in readiness to repel attack.

One of his own family, another siffleur, being added to the imprisoned party, the first-comer was most unfriendly, flying at him, and trying to keep him from food and water.

Another indication of the bird's love of quiet was his annoyance at the hummingbirds, whose ways Mr. Ober was studying, and who flitted about the room all the time. From the first he regarded them with disfavor. Their frivolous manners and their constant humming were not pleasing to him; but when they became so impertinent as to alight on his back, this trifling with his dignity was past endurance; he hissed, and snapped his beak at the elusive little creatures, and finally worked himself into such a rage that he was found completely exhausted, and almost in a dying condition. These continued excitements, indeed, so wore upon his sensitive nature that he did not long survive his extreme passion.

This was the more to be regretted because of the readiness with which he accepted his fate. He became tame in a week after capture, and readily took food from the fingers. From the first he never made the least effort to escape, but seemed perfectly contented, so long as he was alone. It was the presence of intruders—as he regarded them—that he resented so fatally.

One of this most interesting family, Townsend's fly-catching thrush (*Myadestes Townsendii*) is resident in the mountains of Colorado, and it is pleasing to see how the most scientific and the least emotional of chroniclers fall into rapture over his song. "Never have I heard a more delightful chorus of bird music," says one. "The song can be compared to nothing uttered by any other bird I have heard," says another. "A most exquisite song in which the notes of purple finch, wood thrush, and winter wren are blended into a silvery cascade of melody that ripples and dances down the mountain-side as clear and sparkling as the mountain brook," says a third.

Charles Dudley Warner, who found the clarin a favorite cage bird in Mexico, says of his song (in "Mexican Notes"): "Its long, liquid, full-throated note is more sweet and thrilling than any other bird note I have ever heard; it is hardly a song, but a flood of melody, elevating, inspiring as the skylark, but with a touch of the tender melancholy of the nightingale in the night."

XIII.

INCOMPATIBILITY IN THE ORIOLE FAMILY.

One whole year I entertained in my bird-room an individual of strongly marked character, an orchard oriole. Wishing to study his habits, I put a pair of this species into a big cage, hoping they would live happily, as did other couples in the room at the same time. The pretty little yellow and olive dame was amiable enough,—she could live in peace with any bird in the room; but her comrade rebelled against the decrees of man. He was an autocrat; he intended to have his house to himself, and, more, he purposed to appropriate any other residence he chose to select, whoever might claim it. Hostilities began the moment the door was shut upon them; he drove her away from the food-cup, he fought her over the bathing-dish, he answered her sweet call with a harsh "chack" or an insulting "huff," he twitched her feathers if she came near him, and gave her a peck if she seemed to be having too easy a time. Withal, such was his villainous temper that he desired a victim to abuse, and never let her out of his sight for two minutes, lest she should enjoy something he could deprive her of. She was of a happy temperament; she contented herself with what was given her. If she could not have pear, she cheerfully ate bread and milk; while if my lord could not have pear, he would starve. She had large dark eyes, and soft, delicate colors, with legs and feet the tint of light blue kid; but her liege lord was in the immature plumage of the second year, with black mask covering his small eyes.

IN THE LOOKING-GLASS.

Hardly were the two orioles let out into the room when they began to investigate the wonders about them: one flew to the fringe of a window-shade, and hung head down while trying with sharp beak to pry open the cords; the other devoted itself to unraveling the mysteries of books and boxes, very soon learning to open both with the same prying instrument. The slats of the blinds were appropriated as ladders to run up and down, and every few moments one disappeared in some hole, never hesitating to creep through the smallest opening. Madam went up out of sight among the springs of a stuffed chair, while her mate set himself the task of pulling out the stitches of embroidery on a toilet cushion, with perfect success. Having exhausted this amusement, he looked about for new worlds to conquer, and soon found sundry holes in the wall-paper, where I suppose nails had been driven, though they were so hidden by the confused pattern that I could not see them. Before the walls he hovered slowly, and the discovery of an opening was the signal for work. One claw inserted under the broken edge of the paper was perch enough, and the first intimation of the mischief was the falling of bits of plaster and fluttering fragments of paper. Of thus amusing himself he could never be cured, and many unsightly places remained to tell the tale. While the head of the family disfigured the wall, his little spouse found occupation in working at a paper covering the cage of a gentle bird who specially disliked intrusive neighbors. First she pulled out the pin that held it in place, took it under a toe, and tried to wrench the head off; failing in this, she passed it through her beak back and forth as she did a worm, evidently to reduce it to a softer condition. Finding the pin intractable, she dropped it, and turned her attention to the paper; tearing off bits, peeping under it, and constantly worrying the peace-loving owner, until a roof of enameled cloth, securely fastened by sewing, was provided for him.

The only one in the room whom the unlovely bird found it impossible to annoy was the oriole he saw in the looking-glass, and he never gave up trying to reduce even him to a proper state of meekness. Whenever he caught sight of his reflection he was furious: he strode across the lower support, bowing and posturing; then flew up against the glass, touching it with breast and claws, and beating his wings against it. Failing, of course, to seize the enemy, he peered eagerly behind the mirror, then returned with fresh rage to the charge in front. After a while I placed the glass at such an angle that he could not see himself from below. Instantly he alighted on a basket that hung conveniently near, ran to the end where he could stretch around and see his face, then to the other end from which he could look behind, uttering at the same time a loud cry. This also he kept up till I removed the basket. A day or two later, the discovery of a hand-glass standing on a table gave opportunity for a repetition of the performance. He attitudinized, drooped his wings, beat against it, hopped quite over it, touched the glass many times with his beak, and at last circled round and round, going into a rage whenever he reached the front, and springing suddenly around, as if to seize the elusive enemy behind. It was a strange exhibition of passion, very droll if it had not been painful to see. After that the glasses were covered.

Repose of manner was unknown to the orchard oriole; he could never wait a moment for anything. If he wanted to bathe, he plumped into the dish, whether it were empty or not; thus he often surprised a more dignified bird by bouncing in beside him and splashing as though no one else were in sight. In fact, the bath was a constant subject of dispute; he was very fond of it, and the sound of dashing water was always irresistibly tempting to him. If he were shut into his cage with no other amusement, he indulged in gymnastics on the roof, running about, head down, on the wires, as readily as a fly on the ceiling, and often hanging by one claw, swinging back and forth, as if to enjoy the upside-down view of the world. If he stood still two minutes on a perch he was usually asleep; and both of these birds indulged in daytime naps, in which they buried their heads in their feathers, exactly as they did at night.

The lord and master of this household was extremely fastidious in his fare. Mockingbird food he despised, bread and milk he left to his cage mate, apples were too hard to please him; nothing appealed to his taste except the tenderest of Bartlett pears, and of these he condescended to eat one a day. After a while, in his trampish fashion of prowling about in other birds' houses, he discovered that mockingbird food was not so bad; and although he scorned it at home, he soon spent half his time in going from cage to cage, pulling over the food-supply, and selecting dainty bits for his own delectation. Naturally, he had many encounters with insulted proprietors, and some narrow escapes from a pecking; but he accepted these little episodes in the spirit of the tramp, regularly poached upon his neighbors, and nothing would keep him out of others' cages, or convince him that his own dish was as well supplied as any. The truth is, he seemed to be devoured by a fear that some one was better provisioned than he; and this feeling went so far that in the cage of a seed-eater he ate seeds, though since he did not take off the shells he was obliged to throw them up in a ball somewhat later. Like many other birds, the orioles were fond of huckleberries, which they ate daintily, driving their sharp beaks into a berry, and holding it under one toe while they neatly extracted the pulp, thrusting far out their long white tongues in the operation.

Meal-worms—the choice morsels of the bird-room—came near driving the oriole wild. It was natural for him to take one under his toe, and pull off small bits till all was eaten, but his greed made this way very distasteful. How could he be satisfied with a slow manner, while thrushes and bluebirds took one at a gulp, and were ready for more? He could not; he put himself in training, and in a few days could bolt a worm as quickly as anybody. Now it became the object of his life to secure them all for himself. He was so quick in movement that he had no difficulty in swooping down upon every one that was put out, before more leisurely birds had stirred a feather. When he was absolutely incapable of swallowing another, he continued to seize them, kill them by a bite, and drop them on the floor. Nobody cared for dead worms, and thus the selfish fellow managed, as long as he was allowed, to deprive every bird in the room of his share. The remedy was simple: his door was closed till the other birds had eaten, and he pranced back and forth before it, actually squealing with rage, while they disposed of the dainties in their own natural way.

The dearest delight of this bird, however, was one which no other in the room shared,—catching flies. Observing that he tried to get one on the outside of the window-frame, I thought I would indulge him; so the next morning, before the cages were opened, I raised the windows. As I anticipated, two or three flies came in. The oriole saw them in an instant, and was frantic to get out. When his door was unclosed he at once gave chase, and never rested till every fly was caught and eaten. He hunted them up and down the windows with great eagerness, but never followed them back into the room, though of course, as they could not keep away from the light themselves, they all fell victims sooner or later. After that several flies were allowed to come in every morning, and no sportsman, of whatever size, was ever keener after his prey, whether fish, fox, or tiger from the jungle.

The little dame liked flies too, and if one came near her did not hesitate to appropriate it, although it brought her mate upon her "like a wolf on the fold." The two had once a funny time with a very large fly which fell into the hands —or beak—of madam. The victim did not submit with meekness; in fact, he protested in a loud voice. This at once attracted the attention of the master, who flung himself furiously at his usually amiable spouse, to snatch it from her. She did not give it up, but flew away, he following closely, and the fly buzzing madly all the while. Round and round the room they went for some time, till he was tired and gave up, when she alighted and tried to dispose of her prize, which was, after all, rather embarrassing to her. The insect was large, and she seemed afraid to put it under one toe, as usual, lest she should be attacked and have to fly suddenly, and so lose it. When she did make the attempt at last, her movements or his strength caused a slip somewhere, and away he went, buzzing louder than ever in triumph. This sound again roused the hunter's instinct, and both orioles flew wildly after that noisy creature, which took one turn around the room, then alighted on the top of the lower sash of a window, and passed quickly down the hole made for the window-cord. The orioles in chase of this slippery fellow, seeing him outside, came bang against the glass, and then dropped to a perch, looking rather foolish.

THE FLY ESCAPED.

Very soon after these birds were at home in the room, the female began to sing a low and sweet song of considerable variety. The male confined his utterances to scolding and "huffing," and he tried to silence her with a peck, or by making ostentatious preparations for a nap, in which curious way many birds show contempt. But she did not often sing at home. She preferred a perch the other side of the room, where she sat down, her breast feathers covering her toes, threw her head up, and turned it from side to side (perhaps looking for the enemy always ready to pounce upon her), as she poured out the pleasing melody. Not a note of song came out of his throat till weeks afterwards, when her presence no longer disturbed him, and spring came to stir even his hard heart.

Matters culminated, in this ill-assorted union, with a tragedy. He began a bully and a scold; and so far from being mollified by her gentleness, his bad temper increased by indulgence, until he absolutely prevented her from eating, bathing, or entering the cage when he was about. At this point providence—in the shape of the mistress—interfered, bought a new cage as big as the old one, and, in the summary way in which we of the human family dispose of the lives and happiness of those we call the lower animals, declared a divorce. This was agreeable to the female, at least. She entered her solitary cage with joy, and ate to her satisfaction, but not so well pleased was the tyrant; he wanted an object on which to vent his ill-humor, and it grieved his selfish soul to see her happy, out of his reach, with table spread as bountifully as his own. He usurped the new cage; she retired contentedly to the old. Still he was not suited, for the old one was nearer the window; so he tried to occupy both, and drive her away altogether. So outrageous did he become that finally he had to be shut into one cage before she could enter the other. It was curious, on these occasions, to see the care with which she examined the door of his cage, to be sure that he really could not get out, and the satisfied air with which she finally went home; even then she ate at the point of the bayonet, as it were, he raging from side to side of his cage, as near to her as he could get, and scolding furiously. This could not go on forever, and the most watchful care was not able always to protect her without making prisoner of one. It was the middle of winter, and she could not be set free; but if I had suspected how far his tyranny would go, I should have removed one of them to another room. To my deep sorrow, I found her dead one morning, and her body so thin I was sure she had been worried to death.

A BAD TEMPER.

Naturally, I did not love the brutal bird who had teased another out of her life, but I certainly looked for an improvement in his temper now that he had no one to vex his sight. I looked in vain. He was more savage, more of a tramp and poacher, more of a scold, than ever. He even went so far as to huff at the sparrows outside the window. He never entered into the feelings of his neighbors in any way; when every other bird in the room was excited, alarmed, or disturbed, he alone remained perfectly unconcerned, exactly as if he did not see them.

During the latter part of that winter I was interested to see a curious provision of nature for an emergency. The oriole had a serious affection of one hind-toe, which swelled, turned white, and was evidently so painful to use that he alighted on the other foot, holding this one up. After a few days I noticed him using his foot again; there was a hind toe all well, and the disabled one above the new one, quite out of harm's way. It looked as if it were going to fall off, and I did not know but the universal Mother had provided a new toe; but on close examination I found that one of the three front toes had turned back to take the place of the useless member. Thus relieved, it became well, the front toe returned to its proper place, and the bird was all right again.

Now spring came on, and the oriole began to sing, strange, half-choking sounds at first, interspersed with his harshest notes, as if he were forced to sing by the season, but was resolved that no one should enjoy it as music, and so spoiled it by these interpolations. I found afterwards, however, on studying his wild relatives, that this is their customary way of singing. Now, too, queer little spots began to appear in his plumage, dots of bright reddish chestnut, first on one side of the breast, then about the tail coverts, till after a month he looked like patchwork of the "crazy" sort. All this time his song was gaining in strength and volume, till by the first of May he could outsing any bird in the room.

UTTERLY UNLOVELY.

To outdo in some way was his delight, and he regularly discomfited the singers and silenced the gentle ripple of thrush music in the house by his loud carol. Later, the weather became settled, the well and perfect birds were given their liberty, and he had the bird-room to himself, the only utterly unlovely bird I ever knew.

The relations of a pair of Baltimore orioles at the same time were not much more harmonious; but the little dame being more spirited than her neighbor, things arranged themselves differently.

I introduced the pair by the rather summary process of putting both into one large cage. She had suffered at the hands of mankind, and her plumage was in a terribly draggled state; and clothes have as much to do with self-respect in the feathered world as in our own. Her condition of general wreck was so complete as to leave her without a tail,—the last stage of respectability. She was depressed in spirits, and at first did not gainsay the dictation of the bird already in possession. He drove her away from the food-dishes, denied her a place on his perch, and in fact set up for lord and master, and she submitted for a time.

It was amusing to see these birds trying, on the first evening, to settle the question of sleeping-quarters. As usual, the mind of the male was made up, and he planted himself in the darkest corner of the upper perch away from the window, shook himself out, and considered the matter decided. The meek little new-comer did not aspire to his corner, but she ardently desired a place on that farther perch, and after he became quiet she resolved to try for it. Too modest to approach it in the natural way, from the lower perches, she scrambled up the wires of the cage, and shyly came on from the back. The autocrat was not asleep, and the instant her foot touched it he bounced across the cage to the other upper perch. He evidently expected that she would be put to shame in her surreptitious attempt to share his perch, and would at once retire to her proper sphere; but he was mistaken. So far from being embarrassed by his displeasure, she calmly accepted the relinquished position, and prepared for sleep. This was far from satisfactory to his majesty, and he jumped back as suddenly as he had gone; whereupon madam dropped to the floor. But, with true oriole persistence, in a moment she tried it again, going as before up the wires. Again the annoyed oriole deserted his post, and, disappointed in the effect, returned; once more, also, rather disconcerted, she descended to the floor. Not to stay, however. She was as set in her way as he was, and to sleep in that corner was her determination. This curious seesaw performance was reënacted far into the twilight with amusing regularity, but how they finally settled it I could not stay to see.

SHE REBELLED.

The unfortunate condition of the female kept her in subjection a few days, and then she rose superior to clothes, and quietly rebelled. The possession of the bath was the first disputed point. There she took her stand, bowed and postured on the edge, while he splashed unconcernedly in the tub; and the next time she went so far as to remain in the water and keep on bathing, while he assumed the offensive on the edge. After trying in vain to awe or terrify her, he actually plumped in beside her, and they spattered and fluttered side by side, as if they were inseparable friends. The oriole, however, had learned a lesson. He recognized a kindred spirit, and henceforth they lived peaceably together, in a sort of armed neutrality. No quarreling disgraced their house; each went on in his own way, and the other did not interfere.

One had no right to expect sociability between a pair living in mere tolerance of each other, and yet I was disappointed that they did not talk together. I wanted to hear them, but I listened in vain for weeks. In sight or out of sight, it made no difference; they were the same taciturn couple, each occupied in its own way, and never exchanging a note. But at last I caught them. At night, during the winter, each cage was closely wrapped in a thick, warm cover, and before this was taken off in the morning I began to hear low murmurs from the orioles. One spoke in a complaining tone, as if it said, "Why do you treat me thus?" and the other uttered a regular oriole "chur-r-r." In time the sounds grew louder, and I noticed in the querulous tone great variety of pitch, inflection, and duration of note, accompanied often by a hopping back and forth, as if the listener were inattentive. Wishing to see as well as hear this little domestic drama, I took care the next night to arrange the covering in such a way that I could peep in without disturbing it. Then I saw the lordly Baltimore on the middle perch, leaning over and looking at his mate on the floor. He addressed her in a tone so low that it was scarcely audible at the distance of one foot, and she replied in the fretful voice I have spoken of. Then he began hopping from perch to perch, occasionally pausing to take his part in the conversation, which was kept up till they saw me.

A NEW SONG.

Not all the time of the beautiful orioles was passed in contentions; once having placed themselves on what they considered their proper footing in the family, they had leisure for other things. No more entertaining birds ever lived in the room; full of intelligent curiosity as they were, and industriously studying out the idiosyncrasies of human surroundings in ways peculiarly their own, they pried into and under everything,—opened the match-safe and threw out the contents, tore the paper off the wall in great patches, pecked the backs of books, and probed every hole and crack with their sharp beaks. They ate very daintily, and were exceedingly fond of dried currants. For this little treat the male soon learned to tease, alighting on the desk, looking wistfully at the little china box whence he knew they came, wiping his bill, and, in language plain enough to a bird-student, asking for some. He even went so far, when I did not at once take the hint, as to address me in low, coaxing talk of very sweet and varied tones. Still I was deaf, and he came within two feet of me, uttering the half-singing talk, and later burst into song as his supreme effort at pleasing or propitiating the dispenser of dainties. I need not say that he had his fill after that.

On the 24th of April spring emotions began to work in the oriole family. The first symptom was a song, so low it was scarcely heard, though the agitation of the singer, with head thrown up and tail quivering, was plainly enough seen. As it grew in volume from day to day, it proved to be totally different from the beautiful oriole strain of four or six notes, so familiar during the nesting season. It was a long-continued melody, of considerable variety, with an occasional interpolation of the common scolding "chur-r-r." After about a month of this lovely chant, the usual June carol was added, and from this time he sang the two. Both birds also treated us to the several calls we are accustomed to hear in the orchard in that perfect month.

Shortly following the beginning of the second and more familiar song, a change appeared in the relations of the pair. The male assumed the aggressive, and became rather violent in his attentions. He drove his mate around the room, and when he cornered her they indulged in what must be called a "clawing match," upon which he flew away with a loud song, as though he had won a victory. When this performance had gone on a few days, she began to show a disinclination to go home, took possession of another cage whose owner was amiable, and finally turned upon her rough wooer, as I suppose he must be named; though if I had not seen a similar style of courtship among the orchard orioles I should hesitate to give it that name. One morning she rose in her might to put an end to all this persecution, and I saw her on the war-path, pursuing him with open beak; but after fleeing a moment, he turned and flung himself upon her so savagely that both flew violently against the window, which they had not touched for months, being perfectly aware of the obstacle there. However, he changed his manners, and I heard much low, sweet talk in the cage, such as he had used to coax me for currants. She listened, but said nothing. I neglected to say that meanwhile she had replaced her scraggy feathers and grown a fine tail.

FREE AT LAST.

Another time I saw the two orioles on top of a cage, six or eight inches apart. First she stretched up and faced him, uttering a peculiar cry, a single note of rich but mournful tone, and then she bowed again and again, constantly repeating the call. He posed, turned this way and that, evidently aching to fly at her. At last she flew, and he followed to another cage, where the performance was repeated. Then came a mad chase around the room, which she ended by slipping behind a large cage.

For some days these scenes were frequent, and I began to feel myself a jailer; so one morning they were carried to the country, where sparrows would not mob them, and set at liberty to pursue their wooing, if such it were, in freedom.

CPSIA information can be obtained
at www.ICGtesting.com
Printed in the USA
LVHW110106010920
664725LV00011B/897